"You don't have to be so crude," she said.

"I call it like I see it. You dolled yourself up then set your sights on me. After you got what you wanted, you walked away without a backward glance."

Miffed, Beth planted her hands on her hips. "And I see it like this... You approached me in the bar, and unlike my husband I at least waited for my divorce to become final before I took a walk on the wild side." She narrowed her eyes. "And the reason I dolled myself up was because men like you never give women like me a second glance."

"What are you talking about?"

She spread her arms wide. "When it comes to passion and desire I'm no man's fantasy."

"You don't think very highly of yourself." She would have fled, if her only escape route hadn't been blocked by a broad-shouldered cowboy. "I think we should—"

"Pretend that night never happened," she said.

Forgetting her evening with Mack was the last thing she wanted to do, but she didn't dare tell him that unless she cared to keep torturing herself.

"Fine," he said. "We'll act as if we've never met before."

Dear Reader,

Like the other Cash brothers, Mack attracts his fair share of female attention, and being the lead singer of the Cowboy Rebels makes him a favorite with the buckle bunnies. But Mack's getting tired of the single life and he's ready to find the right woman—that is, after one more fling with a woman who won't share her last name.

The fun begins when the mystery woman turns up as a guest at the Black Jack Mountain Dude Ranch where Mack's a wrangler, except she's not a buckle bunny anymore—she's exactly the kind of woman Mack's looking to settle down with. He's willing to give Beth a second chance, but she's not on board with his plans for a committed relationship. The happy-ever-after Mack envisions for them might be hijacked by Beth's insecurities and her belief that she can't give Mack the family he's always wanted. I hope you enjoy watching Mack and Beth struggle to find their way as a couple, and when you reach the end of the book you'll be a believer like Beth that the true meaning of family is more than biology—the meaning of family is all in the heart.

If you missed any of the previous Cash Brothers books, they're still available for purchase online: *The Cowboy Next Door* (July 2013), *Twins Under the Christmas Tree* (October 2013), *Her Secret Cowboy* (February 2014) and *The Cowboy's Destiny* (May 2014). To keep up-to-date on my books, contests and writing news, please visit my website, www.marinthomas.com, where you'll find links to all my social media hangouts.

Happy Ever After...The Cowboy Way!

Marin

TRUE BLUE COWBOY

Marin Thomas

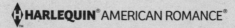
HARLEQUIN® AMERICAN ROMANCE®

ISBN-13: 978-0-373-75530-1

TRUE BLUE COWBOY

Copyright © 2014 by Brenda Smith-Beagley

Printed in U.S.A.

ABOUT THE AUTHOR

Marin Thomas grew up in Janesville, Wisconsin. She left the Midwest to attend college in Tucson, Arizona, where she earned a B.A. in radio-TV. Following graduation she married her college sweetheart in a five-minute ceremony at the historic Little Chapel of the West in Las Vegas, Nevada. Over the years she and her family have lived in seven different states, but they've now come full circle and returned to Arizona, where the rugged desert and breathtaking sunsets provide plenty of inspiration for Marin's cowboy books.

Books by Marin Thomas

HARLEQUIN AMERICAN ROMANCE

*The McKade Brothers
**Hearts of Appalachia
***Rodeo Rebels
§The Cash Brothers

This book is dedicated to The Cash Brothers Cowgirl Posse...Denise, Susan, Nancy, Renee, Teresa, Sabrina, Gaby, Linda and Kim... Thank you for your help in spreading the word about The Cash Brothers series—you ladies rock! But most of all... thank you for your friendship.

Prologue

Two could play the cheating game.

Except it wasn't really cheating, because Beth Richards and her husband, Brad, were officially divorced. Earlier in the afternoon they'd met at the lawyer's office to sign the papers. Afterward, Beth had gone on a shopping spree.

She adjusted her brand-new Victoria's Secret push-up bra and fluffed the fake brown hair extensions that made her look twenty-one instead of thirty-one. She studied herself in the ladies'-room mirror and decided her lips could use a second coat of Ravish Me Red, then cursed her trembling fingers when she rummaged for the tube of gloss in the rhinestone-studded clutch.

You've come this far, don't you dare chicken out.

She swiped fresh color across her lips and smoothed nonexistent wrinkles in her retro Western shirt. She looked nothing like a financial consultant for a top-rated investment firm and everything like the girls in the bar hoping to snag a cowboy.

Maybe if you'd dressed sexier for Brad, he wouldn't have strayed.

And if Brad had remained faithful, he never would

have gotten Beth's boss pregnant and then decided that he *did* want to be a father after all.

Beth shushed the voice in her head and recalled her therapist's words. *Your husband's infidelity is his problem. You didn't cause it.*

But her sterility *was* Beth's problem and in the end, the reason her husband had filed for divorce. Sadly, had he not contacted a lawyer first, who knows how many months would have passed by before Beth discovered Brad was cheating on her? At least she understood the real reason behind the extra customer accounts she'd been asked to manage—Sara had hoped to keep Beth at the office on weekends while she snuck around with Brad.

Beth should have known something like this would happen after the way she'd caught Sara ogling Brad at the July Fourth company picnic nine months ago. Instead, she'd believed her sports-anchor husband's claim that sexy women were a dime a dozen but when it came to marriage, he wanted a down-to-earth woman like her. When Brad had proposed to Beth, she'd told him that she couldn't have children, and he swore he didn't care.

The schmuck had done an admirable job hiding his true feelings the past five years, but the truth had come out during the divorce negotiations. Brad admitted he'd only married her to secure his job at the station when he'd heard rumors that the executives weren't happy with his playboy image and might not renew his contract.

After Brad established himself as a settled man with his viewing audience, he'd decided having a family would move his career up the ladder. He was a user and she hated that she'd been taken in by his handsome face and playboy charm. Most of all, she despised him for doing a number on her self-confidence. But tonight she intended to recover it.

I can do this.

Never in her wildest dreams had she believed she was capable of walking into a bar and picking up a stranger. But after Brad's betrayal, she desperately needed to prove to herself that she was still desirable.

The bathroom door opened and a pair of young women wearing stocking caps waltzed in. The chatty Cathies reminded Beth that Christmas was in twenty days, and this year she would not be attending Channel 3's toy drive with Brad. The thought made her sad. Even though she wasn't able to have children of her own, she'd looked forward to handing out gifts at the station. This year she'd sit home alone and watch reruns of *A Christmas Story*. She had considered spending the holiday with her parents in California, but she hadn't gotten up the courage yet to tell them about the divorce.

"Nice belt," the brunette said.

"Thank you." Beth had paid almost four hundred dollars for her outfit—way-too-tight Cruel Girl jeans and a Roar shirt with enough sequins to light up Times Square. Add a rhinestone belt, purse and jewelry to her ensemble and she was pure sex in cowboy boots. Squaring her shoulders she left the ladies' room, wincing when the wall of loud music hit her.

While getting her hair done at the beauty salon she'd overheard the stylists mention the Number 10 Saloon on the west end of Yuma. According to them, the Cowboy Rebels played on Saturday nights and their music was worth the ten-dollar cover charge. Beth had never heard of the band—she preferred classic rock. But what the heck, she'd already had a TV sportscaster in her bed—why not a swaggering cowboy?

She weaved through the tables and returned to her stool at the bar. "Thanks for saving my seat," she shouted at the man next to her. He wasn't much to look at. According to Brad, she wasn't all that special in the looks department, either. She shoved her ex to the back of her mind and watched the patrons in the mirror mounted to the wall behind the bartender. This was her first foray into a country-and-western bar and she was pleasantly surprised by the decor. Used to eating in high-end dining establishments and frequenting upscale hotel lounges, she'd expected a dark, dingy saloon that smelled like spilled beer and men who needed a bath.

To her surprise the interior of the club could have been any frontier bar from the Old West, except that the furnishings were brand new and the place had been decorated for Christmas. A lighted tree stood next to the red-velvet curtains that framed the stage, and giant bows hung on the oil paintings of scantily clad women adorning the walls.

The food menu had been printed on the backs of Wanted posters, and battery-operated lanterns served as the centerpieces on the tables. Wide wooden planks covered the floor and wood beams crisscrossed the ceiling.

The band ended one song and began another. Beth listened to the lead singer belt out "Drink Up and Be Somebody," which reminded her... She tapped an acrylic fingernail on the bar and a third glass of Bordeaux magically appeared. She sipped the wine and focused on the lead singer who'd introduced himself as Mack Cash. As he moved across the stage, his brown eyes and shaggy brown hair screamed T-R-O-U-B-L-E. The kind of trouble she was looking for tonight.

He wore a tight black T-shirt that showcased his muscular chest, and his jeans rode low on his hips, accentuating a trim waist and a flat belly. And the faded denim was torn, frayed and ripped in all the places that made a woman's mouth water.

Oh, yeah, she'd found her man.

Before the night was through, she was leaving the bar with Mack.

A group of women moved closer to the stage, their big breasts bobbing and bouncing for the band's viewing pleasure. Beth's push-up bra helped her figure, but her girlfriends couldn't compete with what was on display.

"Care to dance?"

The question came from behind Beth, and she spun on the stool. Average height, pleasant face, receding hairline, brand-new cowboy hat in hand, a bucking-horse belt buckle, freshly pressed jeans and a Western pearl-snap shirt. The weekend cowboy had tried hard to pull off the look, but he didn't stand a chance in a bar full of real ones.

An invisible string tugged Beth's head sideways, her gaze colliding with Mack's. She stopped breathing when he smiled at her. "I'm sorry," she told weekend cowboy. "I'm with him." She nodded to the band. Now if only she knew how to execute her plan.

You need a clever pickup line.

How about… Hey, cowboy, wanna share my saddle? *Ugh.*

I'll be your Miss Kitty if you'll be my Matt Dillon. *Cheesy.*

The Cowboy Rebels ended their music set and

Mack announced that the band was taking a break. He set aside his guitar, stepped off the stage and headed straight for Beth.

Her pulse sped up as she anticipated a night of revenge sex—even if it did come *after* her divorce.

Mack stopped next to her and she felt the warmth in his eyes clear down to her toes. The cowboy probably flirted with hundreds of women each weekend, yet he made her believe she had his undivided attention. He leaned against the bar, the movement sending a whiff of musk cologne and warm male past her nose.

Oh, boy. She'd bitten off more than she could chew.

"I haven't seen you here before. First time?"

She nodded then silently cursed her dry throat. "Yes. And you?" *Oh, God.* She didn't just ask that, did she? *Get a grip on yourself and stop acting like an idiot.*

"My band's been playing at the bar for a few years." He nodded to her wineglass. "Mind if I join you for a drink?"

"Please." The guy next to Beth had vacated his seat without being asked. Mack slid onto the stool, his knees bumping her thigh. The bartender set a beer in front of him. He nodded to her wineglass. "Can I buy you another?"

Three glasses of wine was her limit. "I'm good, thanks."

His stare grew intense and she resisted squirming. Even when she'd dated hotshot Brad, he hadn't made her feel this off balanced.

"I'm Mack Cash."

"Beth."

"Beth what?"

"Just Beth."

"An Arizona cowboy walks into a bar and takes a seat next to an attractive woman named Just Beth." Mack kept a straight face. He'd noticed Beth the moment she'd entered the bar and had been hoping she wouldn't hook up with another cowboy before he had the chance to speak with her.

"The cowboy gives Just Beth a quick glance then casually looks at his watch." Mack nodded to his timepiece. "She asks…" He waited to see if she'd help his story along and when she didn't, he said, "'Is your date running late?'" Mack shook his head. "'No', the cowboy replies. 'I just got this state-of-the-art watch and I was testing it.'"

Beth's eyes twinkled and her posture relaxed. The muscle in her thigh was no longer as hard as a rock and she'd quit tapping her fingernail against the wineglass.

"Intrigued, Just Beth says, 'What's so special about your state-of-the-art watch?' The cowboy explains, 'It uses alpha waves to talk to me telepathically.'"

She laughed.

"So this Just Beth points at the cowboy's watch and says, 'What's it telling you now?'"

Mack leaned closer to Beth and whispered. "'It says you're not wearing any panties.'"

She faked a surprised gasp. "How did Just Beth respond to that?"

"She said the cowboy's watch must be broken 'cause she's wearing panties."

"And what did the cowboy say?" Beth asked.

"He points to his watch and says, 'Damn thing's an hour fast.'"

Beth's mouth formed a perfect *O* then she snapped it shut and giggled.

Mack glanced at her bare ring finger. "So tell me, Just Beth, do you have a cowboy waiting for you at home?"

"Not anymore."

"If I were to suggest we get to know each other better after the band finishes tonight…"

"I'd say yes."

Score! Mack leaned in close, inhaling her sexy scent. "I'll see you in an hour." He returned to the stage and the band played a set of rodeo songs and he pushed Beth to the back of his mind, focusing on entertaining the crowd. He never wanted to disappoint his fans.

During the week he made decent money cowboying at the Black Jack Mountain Dude Ranch, but it was the income he earned playing music that padded his savings account. His married brothers suggested he use the money to build a house and find a good woman to settle down with. In the span of a little over three years, four of his brothers and his younger sister had tied the knot. Mack and Porter were the only single siblings left in the family.

A part of Mack admitted that he wasn't getting as much satisfaction out of the singles scene but old habits died hard, and he was only willing to give up the nightlife when the right woman came along. He looked over at the bar.

Just Beth's stool was empty.

There went another shot at finding the right woman.

THE LAST PATRONS walked out the door of the Number 10 Saloon and drove off, leaving only a few scattered pickups in the parking lot. Beth sat on the tailgate of one of the trucks, rocking her legs as if she was on a playground swing.

She hadn't been this excited or terrified in longer than she could remember. But she'd never done anything like this before. Maybe she should have indulged in a fourth glass of wine while she'd waited for Mack.

Too late now.

The saloon door opened and the Cowboy Rebels walked outside, carrying their instruments. The group exchanged words then broke apart and each member went to their vehicle. Mack's truck sat in the shadows at the back of the lot, and it wasn't until he got within ten feet of the pickup that he saw her and applied the brakes. A slow smile spread across his face.

"How'd you know this was my ride?" His husky voice poured over her like honey and she shivered.

"The sign on the door."

He rubbed a finger alongside his nose as if embarrassed and nodded to the magnetic sheet displaying a cowboy on a bucking horse and the band's name and website URL printed across the background. "Had those made up a few months ago."

An uncomfortable silence stretched between them, and Beth wondered if she'd read the signals wrong and Mack had only been teasing about sneaking away together after the bar closed. She hopped off the tailgate. "I…umm…"

Mack moved closer until only a whisper of air squeezed between their bodies. His fingers toyed with one of her hair extensions—could he tell it was fake? He tilted his head to the side to avoid bumping her face with the brim of his hat. Then he kissed her.

Sweet mercy.

The intensity of his kiss curled her toes—pure un-adulterated hot, ferocious need. His mouth moved over hers with purpose, and his tongue left no doubt in her mind that he wanted her. She pressed herself against him and buried her hands in his hair, knocking his hat off. Her body had a will of its own and she rubbed the heel of her cowboy boot against the back of his calf.

When he ended the kiss, Beth gasped for air. If things went no further between them than a hot, lusty kiss in the parking lot, she'd go home a satisfied woman. Even so, tonight was about moving on with her life.

"The El Rancho Motel is a few miles from here." The lodge was located near the neighborhood where she and Brad had bought their house.

Mack tucked a strand of hair behind her ear and the gentle gesture tweaked her heart. "You want to follow me in your car or take my truck?"

"I'll follow." There was no reason to give him the impression that she wanted more than a one-night stand. If all went as planned, she'd be gone before he woke in the morning.

He bent over and grabbed his hat off the ground.

She nodded to the white Lexus and he grasped her hand and walked her to the car, then waited for her to sit in the driver's seat. "Are you sure?" His mouth hovered so close to hers, she could feel his breath.

"Very sure." She brushed her lips over his and he groaned.

"Drive safe." He shut the door.

Never in Beth's thirty-one years had she envisioned herself going to a motel with a complete stranger.

Mack isn't really a stranger. He was a popular local

musician, and her gut insisted she had nothing to worry about.

Then again her gut had gotten it wrong with Brad.

Chapter One

"Damned tractor broke down again." Mack's brother Conway entered the bunkhouse and removed a bottled water from the fridge.

"Thought you finished harvesting the pecans last week," Porter said.

"I've got a few acres left." Conway nodded to Mack, juggling fruit. "What's he up to?"

"Merle Haggard is getting ready to run off and join the circus."

"Real funny." Mack caught the pieces of fruit and glared at his brothers. If he wasn't tied in knots over *Just Beth* he might challenge Porter to a scuffle after being called by his proper name.

Grandma Ada had insisted that their mother name all her sons after country-and-western legends because she loved their music. Mack didn't buy the story. No matter what any of his siblings thought, he believed his mother had been dropped on her head as a baby, leaving her judgment permanently impaired. He and his brother Willie Nelson had taken nicknames after they'd entered kindergarten, and the teasing led to playground fights and weekly trips to the principal's office.

"Can you guys be serious for a minute?" Mack asked.

"Sure," his brothers answered in unison.

Porter Wagoner was still single like Mack, and Conway Twitty, who everyone had believed would remain single the longest, had been the second Cash brother to marry. He was already the father of six-year-old twins with another set on the way early next month. Maybe Mack should talk to his eldest brother, who always gave sound advice. "Never mind. I'll stop by Johnny's before I head out of town."

"Johnny and Shannon are in Payson at a rodeo," Conway said. "They took little Addy up there to show her off to Shannon's friends."

Fine. "You guys ever have a one-night stand with a woman you could swear isn't a one-night-stand woman?"

The brothers exchanged puzzled glances then Porter spoke. "What are you talking about?"

Mack set the apples and orange in a bowl and paced in front of the TV. "I met this woman at the Number 10 Saloon last month before Christmas when the band was playing a gig there."

"And you went back to her place after the bar closed," Porter said.

"Am I telling this story or are you?" Mack asked.

Porter held up his hands. "Sorry."

"So we make eye contact and—" Mack pointed his finger when Porter opened his mouth "—the sparks are there. We go to a motel—"

"Which one?" Conway asked.

"Does it matter?" Mack scowled. "We're at the motel and while we're becoming acquainted and…stuff, I get this feeling that she's not really who she is. You know what I mean?"

"No," his brothers echoed.

Frustrated, Mack shoved his fingers through his hair. "She dressed like a buckle bunny, but she drank red wine." And she drove a Lexus.

"I've never dated a girl who liked wine," Porter said.

Conway scrunched his brow. "Come to think of it, neither have I. The girls I dated drank beer."

"Did you search for her on Google?" Porter asked.

"I'm not a stalker," Mack said.

"What's her name?" Porter asked. "Maybe I know her."

"Beth."

"Beth what?"

"Just Beth."

Porter and Conway exchanged glances. "Did you get her number?" Conway asked.

Mack's face burned and Porter hooted. "She wouldn't give you her number, would she?"

"No."

"There are hundreds of women who'd fall all over themselves to date a musician," Conway said. "Why are you preoccupied with a one-night stand?"

Mack opened his mouth then thought twice about telling his brothers the truth—they'd laugh him out of the bunkhouse. "Never mind." He grabbed the duffel bag he'd filled with clean clothes. "I'd better get going."

"Isi's put a roast in the oven," Conway said. "Stay for supper. The twins would love to throw the football with you."

That was another thing that bugged Mack—his sister-in-law had taken the last single Cash brothers under her wing after Buck had married Destiny and moved to Lizard Gulch. When Mack had learned that Isi had lost her brothers at a young age, he'd grudgingly accepted her hovering. Meddling women aside, the dude ranch was an hour's drive from the farm, and there was nothing between here and there but a dilapidated ice house that sold year-old beer and stale snacks. "I guess I could eat before I take off."

"Good." Conway headed for the door. "Porter, you're washing the dishes tonight."

"What are you going to do?" Porter trailed Conway outside.

"Work on the tractor."

"You're always tinkering with the tractor." Porter's voice filtered through the open windows. "I don't think there's a damn thing wrong with the engine. You just don't like doing household chores."

"You ever try to help a woman who's eight months pregnant?" Conway's voice began to fade. "It's like facing a charging bull…"

Once his brothers were out of earshot, Mack closed his eyes and envisioned his body entwined with Beth's. He'd had a one-night stand with a woman named Just Beth at the El Rancho Motel.

There was no doubt in his mind that he'd pleased Beth, but there had been something off about her behavior—almost as if going to a motel with a man had been a first for her. When she'd snuggled against his side after they'd made love, he'd wondered if maybe he was ready to settle down.

Except Beth wasn't what he was looking for in a wife—he wanted a girl-next-door type. She was a woman who went to a motel with a man she'd met only hours earlier. Before he'd fallen asleep, he'd asked for her number but she'd refused to give it to him—a first for him. Her rejection had left him with an uncomfortable feeling in his gut.

Why the heck did it bother him that Beth didn't want to see him again? Was he losing his touch with the ladies? Mack popped off the bed, took his duffel and left the bunkhouse.

"Uncle Mack!" Conway's son Javier raced toward him, his brother, Miguel, hot on his heels.

Mack set the bag in the truck bed. "Where's Bandit?" Mack scanned the yard but the dog was nowhere in sight.

"He's in the house." Javier squeezed Mack's thigh. "How come you're never here anymore?"

He ruffled the dark mop of hair. "'Cause my job is far away." He broke free, walked over to the porch steps and picked up the Nerf football. "Who wants the first pass?" Before he had his arm cocked to throw, Miguel took off. He tossed the ball, but the kid missed.

"Javi's up next, Mig."

"Don't throw it too hard, Uncle Mack." The boy ran with his head down—an athlete he was not.

"Here it comes, Javi!" The ball smacked him in the chest, knocking him to the ground. Mack hurried across the yard, worried he'd hurt his nephew. "You okay, Javi?"

"I think so."

"Hey, Javi—" Miguel sat next to his brother "—you almost caught that."

"I know." Javi got to his feet and the brothers exchanged a silent message.

Mack glanced between the boys. "What's going on?"

Mig nodded to Javi then both boys tackled Mack to the ground. A scuffle ensued and they rolled in the dirt, laughing. Mack made a big show of accepting defeat, and the boys straddled his chest and pumped their fists in the air.

The porch door opened, and Conway hollered for them to come eat. The twins scampered away, leaving Mack staring at the blue sky. He and his siblings had grown up without fathers—their grandfather had been their only male role model. Mack had been surprised when his brothers had begun having babies of their own, but after watching Johnny, Conway and Will interact with their kids, Mack had decided just because his father had wanted nothing to do with him didn't mean he couldn't be a good father himself.

He crawled off the ground and brushed at his clothes. Time to quit moping over Just Beth. January had ushered in a New Year and a new resolution to refocus his efforts on finding a woman he could build a life with.

"I HOPE THESE accommodations work for you, Beth." Dave Paxton, the owner of the Black Jack Mountain Dude Ranch twirled his cowboy hat on his finger and tapped the toe of his boot against the tile floor Monday afternoon.

"This will do fine, Mr. Paxton. I appreciate you letting me stay here until I figure out what to do." The ranch owner and Beth's father had been former college roommates at Sacramento State.

"Call me Dave." He cleared his throat. "I'm sorry to hear about your divorce. I doubt your father's too pleased with Brad."

"Actually, Mr.… I mean, Dave…" She dropped her gaze, hating herself for feeling embarrassed when she had nothing to be ashamed of—she hadn't done the cheating. "I haven't told my parents yet."

"Why not?"

Beth didn't know if her father had told Dave about her mother's breast cancer scare, so she didn't go into detail. "Mom's been having a few health issues lately and I'm waiting for the right time to tell her."

"I hope she's okay."

"She's doing fine now." Beth's mother had two biopsies and had finished radiation treatment right after Thanksgiving. With her mom still weak from treatment, Beth had wanted to wait until she was stronger before spilling the beans about her failed marriage.

"Your parents have no idea you're staying at the ranch." It was a statement, not a question.

"Once I figure things out, I'll make a trip home and talk to them." It was the second week of January and she hoped to decide on a game plan for her future by the end of the month. "I'm more than happy to pay for the use of my cabin."

"I don't want your money, but there is a favor you can do for me while you're here."

"Sure, anything."

"I'd like you to take a look at my retirement portfolio. It hasn't made as much money as I'd hoped the past few years, and I'm wondering if I need to change investment firms."

"I'd be more than happy to give you my opinion."

His silver head bobbed. "Good." He grew quiet, his attention drawn to the window. The ranch owner had been distracted from the moment Beth had arrived.

"Is there something the matter?" she asked.

"Millie walked off the job a few days ago."

"Who's Millie?"

"The housekeeper." His face turned ruddy. "Millie and I have been courting for about a year."

"I'm sorry."

His fingers tightened against the brim of his hat. "We've had disagreements before but it's not like her to leave me high and dry."

The ranch housekeeper hadn't been the only one left high and dry. Beth's home had sold within a week of going on the market in mid-December, and she'd had to scramble to put her belongings in storage and find a place to live. Not only had she been forced out of her home, but she'd been forced out of her job. She hadn't been fired, but how on earth could she work for the woman who was about to give birth any day to her ex-husband's baby?

Needing a temporary place to live and lick her wounds, Beth had perused apartment listings when she'd remembered that her father's college buddy managed a dude ranch. Her parents had visited the retreat in the past but Beth had never gone along with them— horseback riding wasn't her thing—but a ranch was the perfect place to hole up and not have to worry about running into her ex and former boss while she contemplated her future. Besides, if she'd remained in town, she'd have been tempted to drop in at the Number 10 Saloon and ask Mack Cash if he was up for a second go-round with her.

"You're frowning," Dave said. "Don't you like your accommodations?"

"No, the cabin is perfect." The place had all the essentials—a TV, queen-size bed, love seat, chair and a private bathroom. The best part of the cabin was the covered porch that offered a stunning view of Black Jack Canyon. "If you don't hear from Millie soon, what will you do?"

"Start interviewing new housekeepers." He walked to the door. "C'mon, I'll show you the rest of the place."

Unpacking would have to wait. She left her purse on the bed next to the suitcase then locked the cabin door and accompanied Dave along the stone path that broke off from the main walkway used by the guests. "How many employees do you have?"

"Two full-time workers and three part-time. You'll meet them at supper." He glanced at Beth. "You're welcome to take your meals in your cabin, but the cowboys are expected to eat with our guests." Dave smiled. "Folks like to listen to their tall tales."

Cowboys. Beth would never hear that word again without thinking of Mack. Even now—thirty-four days after their night at the El Rancho Motel—she couldn't get his image out of her head. She didn't understand how a few hours with an almost complete stranger had left a lasting impression on her. First on the get-her-life-back-in-order list was to forget Mack.

Dave stopped at the adobe cantina and held the door open for her. "This used to be an old mission outpost for Jesuit priests several centuries ago."

Beth spun in a slow circle, taking in the plastered walls and dark wooden beams crisscrossing the ceiling. A large fireplace took up a good portion of the room and resting on its mantel were portraits of Spanish matadors. A pair of sofas and chairs covered in cowhide sat near the fireplace. "It's beautiful."

"This was the main room of the mission. The third

owners of the guest ranch converted it into a saloon and a dance hall."

"Wow, this place is full of history."

"There's information about the ranch in the guest packet in your cabin."

"How many owners has the ranch had?" Beth asked.

"Seven. The land that the ranch sits on used to be part of a three-million-acre grant from the King of Spain to the Ortiz brothers of Mexico."

"How long ago was that?"

"1812. The Gadsden Purchase was signed in 1854, determining the border between Mexico and the United States and the ranch fell inside the U.S. boundaries."

"Who got the land after that?" she asked.

"Former Union Colonel William Sturgis bought the property and renovated the mission. When the Mexican Revolution came, Pancho Villa fired on the main house."

"By main house you mean the building with the lobby and dining room?"

He nodded. "You'll see the cannonball embedded in the stucco wall when we go inside the building."

She wandered closer to the bar and ran her hand over the horse-saddle seats. "Cute idea for stools."

"There have been a lot of famous guests at this ranch over the years."

"Politicians or actors?"

"A few of both. Author Margaret Mitchell wintered at the ranch and Zane Gray also wrote here."

Beth found the information fascinating. "Any presidents?"

"Franklin Roosevelt and Lyndon B. Johnson. We've had a couple of ranch guests through the years report seeing an apparition in this room. You'll let me know if you spot one, won't you?"

"I don't believe in ghosts," she said. Seriously— she majored in business and math in college. She possessed an analytical brain. Logic, not emotion, ruled her actions and decisions, which was probably why she couldn't put her night with Mack behind her. She'd acted out of character—normally she dealt with facts not feelings—but the country-western singer had broken down her barriers and reached a touchy-feely place inside her that she hadn't known existed.

"We're empty right now, but we're full up on the weekend." He walked to the door. "Be sure to take advantage of your stay and go horseback riding."

"I've never been horseback riding."

When they stepped outside, Dave said, "One of our trail hands will give you lessons."

Beth couldn't imagine herself riding a horse. Then again she'd never envisioned herself entering a motel room with a stranger.

There was a first time for everything.

"NEED HELP WITH THAT, HOSS?" Mack stepped into the barn late Sunday afternoon and caught the retired rodeo clown struggling with a wheelbarrow full of soiled hay.

"Best get out of my way unless you want a pile of road apples fallin' on yer fancy boots."

When Mack had taken the job at the dude ranch, the sixty-five-year-old Hoss had been the first employee his boss had introduced him to. The surly man had made it clear the barn was his domain.

Mack stopped in front of Speckles's stall and rubbed the horse's nose. Hoss had been granted the privilege of naming the trail horses—big mistake. The geezer had named the geldings after rodeo clowns—Bim Bom, Coco, Potato, Bubbles, Doink, Flunky, Pooter, Zig and Zag. The only decent name in the whole group was Warrior, and he'd come with the ranch when Dave Paxton had purchased the place ten years ago. "Anything exciting happen here this weekend?"

"Millie ran off." Hoss pushed the wheelbarrow into another stall then took a break.

"What do you mean she ran off?"

"Just up 'n' left." Hoss sat on a hay bale and drank from the water bottle he pulled out of the back pocket of his sagging Wranglers. After guzzling half the liquid he belched. "Didn't leave no note. Nothin'."

Mack knew the feeling. He'd woken alone in bed the morning after at the El Rancho Motel. Beth had left while he'd been asleep—the scent of her perfume on the bed sheets the only evidence she'd been there.

"What's the boss going to do?" Mack asked. "He's got that group of businessmen coming in from New York on Friday."

"He was givin' a gal a tour of the place earlier." Hoss shrugged. "Maybe she's the new housekeeper."

"Let's hope." Mack was willing to do a lot of things at the dude ranch, but he refused to change bedsheets. "How's the boss taking it?" Everyone knew Dave and Millie were sleeping together.

"He doesn't say much, but I figure he's hurtin'." Hoss spit tobacco juice at the ground. "Can't never trust a woman. They ain't ever who you think they are."

Hoss was speaking from experience. His wife had left him years ago when Hoss was still rodeoing. Heartbroken, Hoss rode the circuit, leaving his sixteen-year-old son home alone to fend for himself. At eighteen his son had joined the military and Hoss hadn't seen or heard from him since.

"Maybe Millie will return in a few days. Might have been a family thing."

"Millie ain't got no family." Hoss stood, the old bones in his bowlegged hips creaking.

"Wait here." Mack rolled the wheelbarrow out of the horse stall.

"Get yer hands off my damned horse shit."

"Settle down, old man, before you work yourself into a heart attack." Mack wheeled the 'barrow out a side door and dumped the soiled hay into a compost pile behind the barn. When he returned, he caught Hoss rubbing his twisted fingers and knobby knuckles—leftover souvenirs from his rodeo career.

Hoss grabbed the 'barrow. "You competin' in the Rattlesnake Rodeo at the end of the month?"

The Rattlesnake Rodeo raised money for the only medical clinic in Rattlesnake, Arizona. The closest town with a hospital was four hours west in Tucson. The residents of Rattlesnake depended on the clinic for most of their medical needs. "Yeah, I'll probably enter."

"Yer brothers gonna ride, too?"

"Don't know. Except for me and Porter, they're all married now and busy with their families."

"Might find a wife at the rodeo." Hoss snorted as he pitched soiled hay into the barrow.

"Sorry, Hoss. No buckle bunnies for me." When Mack married, he wanted a down-home girl. Beth's face flashed before his eyes… Why did she have to be like the other women who came to his concerts and just wanted a piece of him? Mack had dreamed of being a musician all his life, but lately the warning *be careful what you wish for* rang through his brain far too often.

He was tired of loose women fawning over him. He was twenty-nine and he'd made a promise to himself that by his thirtieth birthday he'd have found his forever woman.

That wasn't going to happen if he couldn't forget his one-night stand with Just Beth.

Chapter Two

An hour ago Dave had informed Mack that a guest—the daughter of a former college buddy—wanted a horse-back-riding lesson. He checked his watch. She should be here any moment. Mack made sure the saddle on Speckles fit snug in case the horse decided to sprint after a desert jackrabbit. The mare's spirited personality made her his favorite.

"You behave on the trail, you hear?" Speckles's ears twitched and he rubbed the animal's nose. "No showing off in front of Warrior."

Speckles and Warrior had a love-hate relationship. Warrior developed a crush on Speckles the day she'd arrived at the ranch, but Speckles acted as if she couldn't be bothered with the old gelding. Mack checked his watch again. "C'mon, lady. Where are you?"

"Right here."

He spun, opening his mouth to apologize. The words evaporated on his tongue when the blood drained from the woman's face, leaving her skin as white as Elmer's school paste. Worried she'd faint, he stepped forward but she hastily retreated. If she toppled over, he hoped she hit her head on the edge of a hay bale and not the concrete floor.

Eyes wide, she gaped at him. He must remind her of someone—maybe a dead someone. Her lips parted then pressed closed as if her voice, along with her blood, had drained from her body. Since conversation appeared to be at a standstill he studied her, zeroing in on her mouth. When he noticed the faint scar next to her lower lip, his scalp prickled.

Her brown eyes were the same shape as...and her nose was as straight as... *No.* She was missing the butterfly eyelashes and long hair. His gaze trailed down her body, stalling on her breasts. Heat spread through his gut.

It couldn't be...

"Hello, Mack."

Just Beth? No frickin' way.

Of all the places he'd imagined running into the woman who'd snuck off to a motel with him a month ago, the dude ranch had never been one of them. "What are you doing here?"

She blinked as if in a daze. "I didn't know you worked at the ranch."

No kidding. If she had, she wouldn't have booked a cabin here. "You're a tough lady to find." There. He admitted he'd been looking for her. Now the ball was in her court.

She waved a hand in front of her face—her nails were short and there was no trace of the bold, red polish. Gone, too, were the dangling earrings and sparkly eye shadow. Beth wore no makeup—except for the pink shine on her lips. The woman standing before him had nothing in common with the sexy siren he'd met at the Number 10 Saloon.

"You're busy," she said. "I'll come back later."

Like hell she would. "Stay." He wasn't letting her off the hook that easy. "The horses are already saddled." He led Speckles from her stall, then took Warrior's reins and escorted the animals out of the barn. He stopped next to the horse trough and cupped his hands near Warrior's stirrup. "Put your left foot in here and swing your right leg over the saddle."

Beth hesitated then edged closer and grasped the pummel. When she lifted her leg, he moved his hands beneath her shoe and hoisted her—a little too hard. She pitched forward and he grasped her waist, his fingers biting into her flesh to prevent her from sailing over Warrior's head.

She rocked back, her rump hitting the saddle hard. Warrior shifted in surprise. Wanting to be certain she'd regained her balance, he tightened his hold on her, but she took exception to his touch and attempted to twist free. She teetered toward the opposite side and Mack reached for her shoulder, but his hand landed on her breast—a mound of soft flesh his fingers were intimately familiar with.

A jolt of electricity zapped his body, triggering a flashback of their night in the motel. She made eye contact and the heat in her gaze sent a second shockwave through him. She was a live wire.

Without speaking he hopped on Speckles, took Warrior's reins and guided the horses to the trailhead. They rode in silence. With each passing minute, Mack's frustration mounted. He led the horses off the trail toward a shallow water hole.

"Where are we going?"

The tremor in Beth's voice convinced him that the

bold, gutsy lady he'd met at the bar had been an imposter. "The horses need to rest."

She lifted an eyebrow but didn't challenge him. He hopped off Speckles then dropped the reins on the ground. The mare wandered to the water's edge and drank. "Would you like help getting down?"

"No. I'll wait here until your horse is ready to go."

"My horse isn't going to leave until you and I talk." He crossed his arms over his chest and a stare-down ensued.

"Mack." Beth's eyes pleaded with him. "Do we have to discuss that night?"

Ouch. That she wanted to forget the most amazing few hours of his life hurt way more than a nasty fall off a rank bronc. "You owe me a few answers."

Her brow wrinkled. "I don't owe you anything."

Amused by her stubbornness, he asked, "What's your real name?"

With a resigned huff she yanked her foot from the stirrup and slid off Warrior. As soon as her feet hit the dirt, the horse walked to the pond for a drink. "Beth Richards." She jutted her chin as if daring him to challenge her again.

"Why wouldn't you tell me your last name the night we—"

"Because I never planned on seeing you again."

"You're not married, are you?"

"Not anymore."

Startled, he asked, "Were you married when we—"

"I signed the divorce papers earlier in the day before I showed up at the bar."

"So you were celebrating your divorce that night?"

"Yes."

His stomach knotted. Why was he upset that Beth had used him? He'd approached her in the bar. He'd been the one to invite her to go off with him later that night. Maybe that was the problem—he couldn't reconcile the Beth on horseback with the Beth at the Number 10. "Why the getup?"

"Getup?"

"Fancy clothes, heavy makeup and long hair? You looked like all the other buckle bunnies in the bar."

She gestured to herself. "I doubt you would have left with me if I'd walked into the place looking like…me."

Was she kidding?

She dropped her gaze but not before he saw a flicker of doubt in her eyes. "The horses are done drinking."

The horses could wait. He still had a few questions. "Was everything a lie that night?"

"What do you mean?"

"You said you worked at an investment firm."

"I did."

"You quit your husband and you quit your job?"

Her head snapped up. "I didn't quit my husband. He quit me. As for the job, I didn't have any other choice but to quit."

His question had visibly upset her. "What are you doing here? Hiding from an abusive ex?"

"Brad's not like that. He's too wrapped up in his ego to bother making my life miserable."

Mack was relieved she hadn't been mistreated by her ex. "You still haven't told me why you're here at the ranch."

"I needed a place to catch my breath after the divorce."

"You could have caught your breath in Cancún or Belize. Black Jack Mountain?"

"My parents are friends with Dave. They've visited the ranch several times but I never have." She shrugged. "It seemed like a good place to relax and make plans for the future."

Plans for a future that obviously didn't include him.

"Mack, I'm sorry. I thought you were just a singer in a local band. You never mentioned working at a dude ranch."

He kicked a rock across the ground and cursed. He'd brought up his job after they'd made love, but evidently she hadn't been listening. Maybe he was better off not knowing what that night was all about for her. Obviously, she hadn't been as *wowed* by the sex as he had or she'd have tried to contact him after she left the motel.

He fetched the horses. "How long are you staying?" He might have to find a new job if she intended to hide in her guest cabin indefinitely.

"I don't know." She placed her foot in his hands. "I guess until I figure out where I want to move."

She was leaving—that killed any possibility of the two of them starting over. He helped her onto Warrior, then mounted Speckles and clicked his tongue. He could tolerate Beth's presence until she made plans for the future—if not, he was in big trouble.

THREE DAYS HAD PASSED since Beth had discovered Mack was an employee at the dude ranch—how they'd managed to avoid each other was a miracle in and of itself. Then again, she'd taken all her meals in her cabin to increase her odds of *not* crossing paths with the cowboy. Nights were another story. As soon as her head hit the pillow, Beth's mind raced with thoughts of Mack. And when she finally drifted off, visions of their night in the motel plagued her sleep, and each morning she woke emotionally exhausted.

Twice she'd walked down the path to Dave's office to thank him for the use of the cabin and notify him that she was leaving. But her feet had a mind of their own and she'd ended up meandering away from main ranch quarters as she was doing right now. She stopped at the entrance to the barn then glanced at the parking lot. Mack's truck was missing among the vehicles. Maybe she'd sneak inside and visit the horses.

"Hoss?" She waited for her eyes to adjust to the dimness.

"In the storage room."

She passed by the empty stalls, the scent of fresh hay and grain surprisingly pleasant. "I thought I'd visit the horses but—"

"Jake let 'em out to graze."

She exhaled quietly.

"You bored, missy?"

"Maybe a little."

"Mind if I ask a personal question?"

Other than introducing themselves, she and Hoss hadn't exchanged more than a "thank you" or "you're welcome" all week. "Sure."

"What's goin' on between you 'n' Mack?"

Had Mack mentioned their one-night stand to the ranch hand? "Nothing. Why?"

"You don't eat in the dining hall with the rest of us."

"I've been working right through dinner." That was partially true. One day this week she searched the internet for employment opportunities while she ate her supper.

Hoss's rheumy eyes latched on to her and she worried he could see clear through to her soul. "Mack hasn't cracked a joke all week." He removed a towel from the shelf and wiped his hands. "Acts like a man who's—"

"Hoss, don't you have better things to do than bother the guests?"

Mack lounged in the doorway as if he didn't have a care in the world. How long had he been standing there?

"Guess I'll take a few carrots out to the horses." Hoss left the room, his shuffling footsteps echoing through the barn.

Mack unnerved Beth. She hadn't seen this serious side of him the night they'd met. Then he blinked and for a split second she saw a wounded look in his eyes before it vanished.

"Wait." Could it be that he'd asked for her number because their night at the motel had been more than just sex for him? Beth's heart raced with hope...then dread.

You're not the Beth he took to the motel room.

She rubbed her forehead, feeling a headache coming on. That night had been the worst-best mistake of her life. "Mack, this isn't going to work."

He glanced up, his brown eyes devoid of emotion. "What are you talking about?"

"Us...together at the ranch." She scuffed the toe of her athletic shoe against the floor. "I'll tell Dave that I'm leaving in the morning."

"You don't have to go."

"But you don't want me here." She'd find some other place to hole up. Maybe even return to the El Rancho Motel and rent the same room she and Mack had slept in. It would serve her right after going off the deep end and celebrating her divorce with a night of hot sex with a stranger. That ingenious plan sure had backfired.

"You're right," he said. "But this is Dave's ranch. He can invite whoever he wants here. Even women I've had sex with."

Beth's gut twisted. "I can explain…" *I think.*

"No need. I get it. You were out for sex and—"

She gasped.

"What?"

"You don't have to be so crude," she said.

"I call it like I see it. You dolled yourself up then set your sights on me. After you got what you wanted, you walked away without a backward glance."

Miffed, she planted her hands on her hips. "And I see it like this… You approached me in the bar and unlike my husband, I at least waited for my divorce to become final before I took a walk on the wild side." She narrowed her eyes. "And the reason I dolled myself up was because men like you never give women like me a second glance."

"What are you talking about?"

She spread her arms wide. "When it comes to passion and desire I'm no man's fantasy."

"You don't think very highly of yourself."

She would have fled, if her only escape route hadn't been blocked by six feet of wide-shouldered cowboy. "I think we should—"

"Pretend that night never happened."

Forgetting her evening with Mack was the last thing she wanted to do, but she didn't dare tell him that unless she cared to keep torturing herself.

"Fine," he said. "We'll act as if we never met before."

Beth didn't know if he was serious or if his bruised ego was talking. Ego aside, how were they supposed to act as if they were strangers—they'd touched and kissed each other in places strangers wouldn't dare.

He thrust his hand toward her. Warily she placed her fingers on his callused palm. Her chest tightened at the tiny electrical pulses that skittered up her arm. Now she knew she hadn't imagined that sensation the night in the motel—only it hadn't been their hands rubbing together that had created the electrifying feeling.

His fingers folded over her hand and squeezed gently. "Mack Cash. I'm from Stagecoach and I work as a wrangler at the Black Jack Mountain Dude Ranch. I also play in a country-and-western band called the Cowboy Rebels."

He wasn't joking. "I'm Beth Richards and I used to work for Biker and Donavan as an investment counselor. I'm recently divorced and in the process of deciding whether or not I want to remain in Yuma or move away."

The corner of Mack's mouth lifted in a semblance of a smile. "Nice to meet you, Beth. I hope we can be friends."

This was foolish, but she was at a loss when it came to Mack. "Same here."

He released her hand and she resisted curling her fingers into her palm to trap his warmth from escaping. He tipped his hat then left the storage room. Mack strolled through the barn, forcing one foot in front of the other until he stepped into the sun.

"You 'n' that filly set things straight?"

"It's none of your business, Hoss." He hated shutting the old man out but Mack was too confused about his feelings for Beth. Until he knew exactly what he felt for her, he didn't care for anyone's advice.

"I don't think Millie'll be back."

"Millie has it good with the boss." Even though there was a ten-year age difference between the housekeeper and sixty-eight-year-old Dave Paxton, when Mack had seen the couple together, they'd appeared happy.

"So you don't wanna talk about that missy in the barn, eh?" Hoss said.

"Nope."

"She's watchin' us right now."

Mack stiffened but didn't check over his shoulder. "You won't quit nagging unless you know everything, will you?"

"Figure it's only a matter of time before you spill your guts."

"I met Beth at a bar last month. At least I think it was Beth."

"You ain't sure?"

"She was all sexed up and on the prowl."

"You didn't take advantage of that poor gal, did you?"

Mack scowled. If anyone had been taken advantage of, it had been him. Now that a few weeks had passed and Mack had reflected on that night, he admitted that he'd genuinely liked Beth—probably because she hadn't acted like any buckle bunny he'd been out with before. She hadn't been drunk, boisterous or even giggly. And when he'd looked into her eyes there had been intelligence and maturity—qualities that had been missing from the other sloe-eyed beauties he'd hooked up with in the past. "It wasn't like that."

"Then what was it like?" Hoss asked.

"There was something different about her, and when the evening ended I asked for her number."

"She didn't give it to you."

"Nope."

When Hoss grinned, Mack growled. "What the hell's so funny?"

"She's the first lady who hasn't succumbed to your cowboy charm."

"*Succumbed?* You're using pretty big words, Hoss."

"Whatcha gonna do?"

"Nothing." Beth made it clear that she wasn't interested in cozying up with him during her stay at the dude ranch.

"You gonna let a decent woman like her get away without a fight?"

"If she was so decent, she wouldn't have pretended to be someone she wasn't."

"Maybe she had a good reason."

Lack of self-confidence wasn't good enough in Mack's book. And it didn't change the fact that she hadn't wanted him to contact her after they'd had fun at the motel. "She doesn't want anything to do with me."

"Change her mind."

"What's with you?" Mack frowned. "Why do you care about my love life?"

"'Cause you've been a big mope lately."

"A man can take a moment to think, can't he?"

"He can." Hoss spat tobacco juice on the ground. "But there's a time for thinkin' and a time for doin'." He nodded to the barn. "This is a time for doin'."

Doing what? Mack was so dang confused right now he didn't know which way was up or down. He was pissed at Beth for using him, and even though she'd made it clear she wasn't interested in extending their one-night stand, the gnawing in his gut insisted he still wanted to be with her.

So where did that leave him?

Between being a fool and an idiot.

Chapter Three

"Fine. We'll pretend we've never met before." Beth mimicked Mack's deep voice as she hiked along the walking path.

She was at a loss as to how to deal with the country-and-western cowboy. She'd never had a male friend and found the idea intriguing, but Mack wasn't the kind of man a woman could be friends with—not after she'd seen and touched every inch of his naked flesh.

She conjured up a likeness of him lounging in the motel bed and...

"Look out!"

Startled, Beth stopped walking and glanced up. Good Lord, another few steps and she would have collided with a saguaro cactus. She turned and discovered Mack standing several yards behind her—he'd sneaked up on her without making a sound. "I was hiking." *Duh.* Hoping to distract him so he wouldn't ask why she'd almost walked into a cactus, she said, "It's warm today."

He closed the gap between them. "The weatherman forecasted unseasonably warm temps until the end of next week."

"Well, eighty-five degrees in January is too hot, even for Arizona." Why were they discussing the weather?

Because that's what friends do. Flustered, she focused on the canyon in the distance and ignored the sultry scent of his cologne.

"Dave wanted me to tell you that we're taking Roger Kline and his executives on a horseback ride and eating supper on the trail. José left with the chuck wagon a few minutes ago. Since there won't be a formal meal in the dining room, you're invited to join us."

"Thanks, but I don't want to interfere in an all-guys outing." She'd met the CEO of Kline Properties and his minions when they'd moved into the cabins next to hers.

Mack took off his hat and shoved his fingers through his hair—hair that had felt silky to the touch when she'd held his head steady while she'd kissed him. "I'm bringing my guitar along."

After parting ways last month, Beth had listened to country-and-western radio stations, hoping to find a singer whose voice reminded her of Mack's, but none of them had carried a tune quite like the lead singer of the Cowboy Rebels.

"C'mon, Beth. You've barricaded yourself inside your cabin every night this week."

Barricaded? She'd hoped that by keeping to herself, her infatuation with him would wear off. The way her heart pounded right now indicated that her plan had failed. To be honest, she was tired of staring at the same four walls. What could it hurt to socialize with the ranch guests for a couple of hours? And she'd also like to hear Mack sing again.

"Okay. I'll join the group for supper."

His smile sucked the air out of her lungs. Was he really that pleased she'd agreed to go? No, he's just being *friendly.* He put on his hat and walked off.

This *friends* thing bugged the heck out of Beth. Although tempting, a friendship with Mack Cash would be a bad investment. She'd give their companionship all her effort and energy but in the end she'd be left alone.

Beth returned to her cabin and showered. Deciding what to wear was easy. She'd packed jeans she'd purchased years ago—the denim wasn't as fancy as the pair she'd worn to the Number 10—no bling—but they were comfortable and she could sit on a horse in them. Besides, looking sexy was way down on her list of priorities, as was picking up men or picking up where she and Mack had left off.

Her first priority was figuring out which direction her life was headed.

"THESE ARE THE BEST damned beans I've eaten in years." Roger Kline glanced at Beth. "Pardon my swearing, ma'am."

"No worries." Beth smiled.

"José's the finest ranch cook in southern Arizona," Mack said.

"He sure is quiet." Gerald, a balding man with a potbelly, helped himself to more beans.

When Mack hired on at the dude ranch, Dave had informed him that José didn't know a word of English, but Mack sensed the camp cook understood more than he let on. Mack sat on a log in front of the fire and shoveled another forkful of barbecue into his mouth, while he watched Beth out of the corner of his eye. At first he was glad she hadn't backed out of the group supper—he'd wanted to prove to himself that after a one-night stand they could still be friends. But now he regretted her presence.

He'd been positive he'd had it all figured out—why Beth had stuck in his craw after only one night together. For the past year, Mack had been losing interest in playing the field—hot dates with hot chicks was becoming old, but he hadn't found a woman he'd consider dating exclusively. When Beth had waltzed into the bar, he'd assumed she was another *hot chick*.

Not until they'd slept together had he realized there was something different about her—an innocence that hadn't matched her clothes, hair or makeup. When he'd held her in his arms, he'd sensed she wasn't at all like the other women he'd been with. He'd wanted to get to know Beth better, but he'd woken the next morning alone in the motel room. It had been a hell of a blow to his ego that she'd left without a goodbye.

He'd sat on the edge of the bed feeling disenchanted with the singles scene. His thirtieth birthday was eight months away and he'd hoped by then to be with a woman who would stand by his side through thick and thin. A woman he could build a home with. Have a family with. Grow old with.

He'd left the motel that morning determined to find his forever girl but he hadn't been able to forget Beth and her dolled-up image. And now he knew why he'd been so torn over her—Beth Richards was no buckle bunny. She was a forever girl who'd fallen off the wagon for one night.

Right then Beth laughed at one of the guest's jokes and Mack's gut churned with anger—mostly at himself. She'd used him and had made it clear she wasn't interested in pursuing a long-term relationship, but damned if he still didn't want her.

And that pissed him off.

"You gonna play a song for us, Mack, or sit there and scowl at the fire?" Dave asked.

"Sorry." Mack bolted from the log and reached for his guitar. "You caught me thinking."

"Judging by the look on your face," Dave said, "you've either got money troubles or woman troubles."

The men laughed while Beth scraped her beans into a neat little pile on her tin plate.

"How about a Garth Brooks song." Mack strummed a few notes of "Cowboy Bill" then belted out the lyrics, his mixed emotions about Beth lending strength to his voice. He didn't have to look at her to know she paid attention—the side of his face burned from her stare.

Ted, the eldest of Kline's executives, sang along, and the other men slapped their thighs in rhythm to the music until the final verse.

Gerald clapped loudly and whistled between his teeth. "You've got quite a voice, Mack Cash."

"Is it true," Al said, "your mother named you after Merle Haggard?"

Mack shot Dave a dark look and his boss held up his hands. "Hey, it wasn't me."

"Jake mentioned it when he took us skeet shooting the other day," Al said.

Fortunately for Jake, he had the weekend off or Mack would make the wrangler pay. "It's true. My five brothers and I all got saddled with famous monikers."

"His eldest brother is Johnny Cash," Dave said.

The executives laughed then Roger spoke. "Is Cash your real surname?"

"Cash was my mother's maiden name. She never married any of our fathers."

"Fathers?" Paul, the quietest in the group joined the conversation.

"Each of my brothers has a different father, so my mother put her surname on our birth certificates."

"What are the names of your infamous brothers?" Roger asked.

"Johnny Cash, Willie Nelson, Buck Owens, Conway Twitty and Porter Wagoner."

Al shook his head. "I bet it was tough to live down those handles when you were young."

"You'd bet right." Mack grinned. "Johnny stood up for us until we were old enough to fight our own battles."

"Are you the only singer in the family?" Ted asked.

"Yep. Johnny's the foreman of his father-in-law's ranch. Will works construction, and Conway manages the family pecan farm. Buck moved to Lizard Gulch, a small town near Kingman, and he runs an auto body shop with his wife. Porter is still finding himself."

"With a voice like that," Roger said "you must have more women after you than you know what to do with."

Beth stood. "I'll help José clean up." She vanished behind the wagon.

Roger lowered his voice. "I get a kick out of the way that gal blushes."

"Didn't see a ring on her finger," Al whispered.

The hairs on the back of Mack's neck stood on end. Roger and his four executives all wore wedding bands. They'd better not get the idea that Beth was available for a fling during their stay—she wasn't that kind of girl.

She was that kind of girl with you.

Dave cleared his throat. "Beth's the daughter of my old college buddy."

"What does she do for a living?" Al asked.

For a married man, Al showed too much interest in Beth.

"Beth works for an investment firm." Dave removed the coffeepot from the fire and refilled everyone's cup. "She's enjoying a short break from corporate America."

"You mind if I ask her to review my stock portfolio?" Al nodded toward the chuck wagon. "I'd like her opinion on a couple of investments."

Portfolio, my ass. Mack fisted his hand then rubbed his knuckles against his thigh to keep from throwing a punch at the man. Later tonight he'd warn Beth to keep her guard up with Al and the others.

"My guests are free to do what they want here," Dave said.

Right then Beth returned to the campfire. "Everything's packed and ready to go."

"Beth." Al got to his feet. The middle-aged man was in decent shape but Mack doubted he'd ever fought over a woman before. "I hear you have investment experience. Would you mind meeting with me to discuss my stocks?"

"Beth is busy tomorrow." Mack stood.

Al glanced between Beth and Mack, uncertain what to say.

Beth avoided making eye contact with Mack. "I'd be happy to meet with you before supper."

Dave clapped his hands. "Let's head back."

The men set their empty coffee cups in the dishpan on the wagon's sideboard then walked to their horses. When Beth did the same, Mack made a move to go after her but Dave snagged his arm.

"What was all that?"

"I don't know what you mean."

Dave narrowed his eyes. "What's going on between you and Beth?"

"Nothing. Why?"

"You got defensive when Al asked to meet with her."

Mack nodded to the shadows beyond the campfire. Once they were out of earshot of the group, he said, "You and I both know Al wasn't referring to his stocks when he asked Beth to look over his portfolio."

"If I thought Al was a threat, I'd have stepped in. I'm not going to let anyone take advantage of Beth."

"I don't trust Al not to cross the line with her."

"Beth's a smart woman. She can handle Al." Dave walked off and joined the guests by the horses.

Mack watched the city slickers swarm Beth. His brilliant idea to have her join them for supper so he could get to know her better had sure backfired in his face.

BETH SAT ON the cabin's tiny porch facing Black Jack Canyon and sipped her tea. She marveled at the crazy turn her life had taken in the past year. The emotional highs and lows had exhausted her.

She couldn't remember the last long vacation she'd taken from work or when she'd slept in until seven o'clock in the morning. Her stay at the guest ranch had been a nice change from sitting at her desk staring at a computer screen all day. She hadn't realized how much anger and resentment had built up inside her after she'd discovered Brad had cheated. The daily hikes she'd taken at the ranch had helped expel the poisonous feelings from her body.

"Mind if I join you?"

She jumped inside her skin, almost sloshing tea onto her jeans. "I wish you'd stop stalking me."

"Stalking? I knocked on the front door before I came back here."

She motioned to the chair next to her. "Have a seat."

Mack accepted the invite and propped one boot against the porch rail. They sat in silence. The scent of his aftershave drifted past Beth's nose and she gave up fighting the memory of their night at the motel. Not a day had gone by that she hadn't relived those few hours in his arms. Mack's presence at the ranch forced her to confront her feelings for him when she'd rather leave them be.

"Are you going to tell me what's on your mind?"

"How long were you married?" he asked.

"Five years."

"Where did you meet your ex?"

She'd known Mack would eventually ask these questions. "A friend invited me to her company picnic. I ended up on Brad's softball team." Krista had been an intern at the TV station, and since she didn't have a boyfriend she'd brought Beth to the annual spring gathering.

Mack chuckled, the intimate noise reminding her of the sound he'd made when he'd nuzzled the skin behind her ear and learned she was ticklish. "What's so funny?"

"I'm imagining you hitting a home run and your ex's mouth dropping open."

"Amazing," she said.

"What?"

"I did hit a home run, but the reason Brad's mouth

hung open was because I plowed him over at home plate." She smiled. "He wouldn't get out of my way."

"You've got an athlete's body. He should have known better."

She'd rather Mack tell her she had a siren's body.

He told you that night that you were sexy.

Mack cleared his throat. "I stopped by to warn you about Al."

"Why?"

"Needing investment advice isn't his only motivation for wanting to get together with you."

"I'm sure you're wrong. He's married."

"I don't trust the guy."

"I appreciate the warning, but I can handle Al." She expected Mack to continue badgering her, but he changed the subject.

"Are you originally from Yuma?" he asked.

"No. I was born and raised in San Diego."

"How'd you end up in Arizona?"

"After earning a Master's in finance I received a job offer from Biker and Donavan Investments. They had an opening in their Yuma branch. The starting salary was very competitive and with student loans hovering over my head, I took the position." For the most part she hadn't regretted it. She'd lived frugally and had paid off her school debt in record time. Then she'd met Brad, and after they'd married he was promoted to five-o'clock sports anchor and before she realized it, Yuma had become home.

"What about your family?"

"I'm an only child. My parents still live in San Diego. My father is a retired airline pilot and they travel now."

"I can't imagine growing up an only child."

She didn't want to talk about herself. "Besides the brothers you mentioned earlier tonight, do you have any sisters?"

"One. Dixie. All of us were raised by our grandparents." He took off his hat and set it on his knee. "The men who fathered me and my brothers wanted nothing to do with us, and my mother came and went on the farm as she pleased. None of us kids were close to her. She died before our grandparents passed away."

"Do you like being part of a big family?"

"I don't know any different. You get used to all the chaos that comes with seven kids trying to coexist in a house with one bathroom."

The noise level inside their home must have been impressive.

"Grandma Ada used to threaten to spank our backsides with her big cooking spoon if we didn't stop tearing the house apart." He leaned forward in the chair. "Was it tough growing up an only child?"

"Not really." Her standard answer whenever anyone asked her.

"You know what they say about only children, don't you?" he asked.

"What's that?"

"They end up having a whole passel of kids."

She smiled, but deep inside the old, familiar ache tugged at her.

"I've got one niece, five nephews and my sister-in-law is due to give birth to twin girls the first week in February."

"What are the ages of your niece and nephews?"

"Johnny's daughter, Addy, is only four months old. And Will's son, Ryan, is almost fifteen."

"Fifteen?"

"Will got the girl he took to the prom pregnant his senior year of high school, but she never told him that she'd kept their baby."

"How awful."

"Things turned out okay for them. They got married and they're living in Stagecoach. Buck's wife, Destiny, had a baby boy named Cody last week. Dixie and her husband, Gavin, have a son named Nathan. He's three. Conway's twin sons turn seven this spring."

There was obvious affection in Mack's voice when he spoke about his siblings and their children—more proof that she and Mack weren't meant to have had anything more than a fling.

"I think I'll retire now." She stood and waited for Mack to move—his chair blocked her exit from the porch.

Rather than give her room, he reached for Beth. She saw his arms coming and could have dodged them but she had no shame where this man was concerned. He cupped her face and lowered his mouth. Suddenly, she'd lost track of all the reasons they shouldn't kiss.

Mack's mouth locked on to her lips and a delicious tingle spread through her limbs. The tingles turned into shivers when his tongue asked for entrance. Shame on her, but she gave in—without a fight—opening to his thrusting tongue. Her body had a mind of its own, swaying forward until her breasts pressed against his chest. She felt the pounding of his heart through his shirt— was it her imagination or did their hearts beat as one until he pulled away?

His finger traced the moisture left behind on her lips.

"There's a rodeo next Saturday in Rattlesnake. How would you like to come watch me?"

Head foggy from his kiss she mumbled, "Where's Rattlesnake?"

"East of Tucson."

"I've never been to a rodeo."

"Then it's about time you experience 'the bulls, the blood, the dust and the mud.'"

She rolled her eyes. "I don't listen to country music that often but I recognize a Garth Brooks song."

"You'll fit right in at the rodeo." Mack disappeared into the darkness, leaving Beth wishing she'd fit right into his life.

She pressed her fingertips to swollen lips. Mack had kissed her, all right, but it was all wrong.

Chapter Four

"Ladies and gents, welcome to the seventeenth annual Rattlesnake Rodeo in Rattlesnake, Arizona!"

Fans sitting on the bleachers stomped their boots, the din reverberated through the air. Mack motioned for Beth to precede him up the steps to their seats. They'd arrived at the outdoor arena late due to an accident on the highway, and they'd missed the barrel-racing event.

Gear bag over his shoulder, he followed behind Beth, the swish-sway of her tush hypnotizing him. *Friends. You're just friends.* He'd repeated the mantra in his head often since they'd left the dude ranch. Why was it so difficult for him to let go of that night with Beth? Obviously, she'd put it behind her.

He remembered lying in the dark, her warm breath puffing against the side of his neck as she snuggled with him. What if they'd met under different circumstances? Would she have given him a second look if she hadn't been celebrating her divorce?

Once they located their seats, he leaned close. "I'll give you a tour of the cowboy ready area after the roughstock events." The smell of her perfume—an earthy mix of flowers—drifted past his nose and he closed his eyes. She'd worn the same scent the night at the bar and when he'd caught a whiff of it, his heart had beaten faster. His blood had pumped a little harder. And a certain part of his anatomy had grown hard. He mentally cursed. This wasn't the place to become aroused.

"When do you compete?" she asked.

He checked his cell phone. "In an hour."

"And what event did you say you were in?"

Beth knew nothing about rodeo and he found her ignorance refreshing. "Saddle bronc." He'd considered entering the bull-riding event but had chickened out when he'd read the list of bulls—three of the six had nasty reputations. He didn't like the fifty-fifty odds of drawing one of them, so he'd parked his signature on the saddle-bronc list. Besides, today was all about impressing Beth, not falling flat on his face in front of her.

He motioned to the arena. "The bareback competition is next. Saddle bronc is the same thing except we use a special saddle."

"Where are the rodeo clowns?"

Mack pointed at the men wearing colorful clothes, standing in the cowboy ready area. "They're called bullfighters now. Most of them are retired from rodeo, but don't let their age fool you. They're in better shape than half the cowboys."

"Ladies and gentlemen, are you ready for the bareback competition?" The announcer's voice boomed over the loudspeakers, and applause and whistles filled the air. *"Be sure to check out the white tent in the parking lot where the Rattlesnake Medical Clinic is giving away free samples of their namesake to those who donate their money or their blood."*

"Have you ever eaten rattlesnake?" Mack asked.

"No." Beth wrinkled her nose. "Have you?"

"Yep. Before we leave today, we'll stop by the tent and you can try it."

Her expression turned thoughtful. "Are you donating blood?"

"After I ride."

Beth eyed him suspiciously. "Are you saying that to impress me?"

"I donate blood every year." That he'd impressed Beth proved how different she was from other women he'd dated.

You're not dating Beth.

He didn't need the reminder.

"Turn your eyes to chute number three. Ricky Payson is coming out on Pretty Boy Floyd—a world-class bucker and NFR champion."

Mack pointed to the chute. "Ricky's good. He'll nail this ride."

Beth inched forward in her seat, eyes glued to the cowboy and horse. The gate opened and the bronc jumped forward, kicking out with his back legs before clearing the chute. With each buck, Ricky's backside flew into the air.

Mack quit watching the bronc and focused on Beth's pale face. When the buzzer went off, Ricky vaulted through the air and came down on all fours. He got to his feet and scrambled for the rails as the pickup men cornered the bronc. They released the cinch then the horse peacefully trotted out of the arena.

"It's a whole different world," Beth said.

"What's that?"

"Rodeo."

"Like I mentioned the other night…'it's the bulls, the blood, the dust and the mud.'"

She nudged him playfully and the contact sent an electrical current racing through his chest straight down to his crotch. He closed his eyes and an image of Beth's naked body on top of him materialized.

"Mack?"

"What?"

"The horse's movements looked so violent. Does it hurt?"

"Yes."

Her smile faded. "Then why do you do it?"

"I like challenges." Mack wasn't as hardcore as some of his fellow contenders, but like any cowboy, he enjoyed pitting his skills against a green bronc and seeing who came out on top. Even if his score wasn't good enough to win, if he made it to the buzzer then he claimed victory. "I'd better get going. Do you want to stay here or come with me?"

"Am I allowed behind the chutes?"

"Sure." He took his bag then her hand and led the way out of the stands. He kept a tight grip on her fingers as they weaved through the crowd. Was it common for male-female friends to hold hands? Hell if he knew. His friends had always been guys and the girls had always been…well, girls. Women he'd slept with, dated or chased after.

They stopped behind the chutes where gear bags and cowboys were scattered about. Some of the contenders stood off by themselves, mentally preparing for their rides, while others put on their protective gear and wrapped their wrists, ankles and knees with elastic bandages.

"Well, well, well."

Mack released Beth's hand when he came face-to-face with southern Arizona's rodeo Romeo. "Rodriguez."

The cowboy's attention drifted to Beth, and his smile widened as his gaze roamed up and down her body. "You got a new fan, *Merle?*"

Mack's spine stiffened. He didn't know if he was pissed off Rodriguez was baiting him or angry that Beth smiled back at the bad boy of rodeo.

"C.J. Rodriguez. Beth Richards. C.J. mostly rides bulls."

Beth held out her hand. "Nice to meet you, C.J."

"She's not your usual type." Rodriguez smiled at Beth. "I don't recall seeing you on the circuit."

"This is my first rodeo," Beth said.

"If you're not a rodeo fan, mind if I ask what is it you do?" Rodriguez asked.

"I'm a financial adviser."

"You don't say." Rodriguez glanced at Mack. "You must have won the lottery if you're using Beth's services 'cause you sure haven't won a rodeo in a long while." He snickered at his own joke.

Mack refused to be drawn into a verbal sparring match and encourage the braggart.

"When I claim the national title in Vegas next December—" Rodriquez grinned at Beth "—I'll hire you to manage my winnings."

"If the rest of the year goes anything like the past month," Mack said, "I doubt you'll be headlining at the Thomas & Mack Center this coming December."

"You've gone downhill since you started singing with your band. Can't recall when I last saw your name in the top ten."

"I'm not making a living at rodeo, am I?" Mack said.

Rodriguez jutted his chin. "Maybe if we'd all been born with stupid names like Merle Haggard we'd be able to sing our way to the bank."

Beth stiffened next to Mack. This conversation was over, but he couldn't resist one more taunt. "You keep running off at the mouth and I'll make sure you're too sore to sit a bull."

"Out of all the Cash brothers—" Rodriguez stepped closer "—you were the one who always threw the first punch."

The nuisance wanted to make a fool out of Mack then swoop in and steal Beth—just to prove he could. *Over my dead body.*

"Back off, Rodriguez."

"Does she know about your fighting days?" Rodriguez nodded to Beth. "Merle Haggard, here, spent more than a few nights in jail for brawling."

On four occasions his brothers had had to bail him out—the bull rider made it sound like Mack had lived half his life behind bars.

"You're more like your namesake than you want to believe except you haven't landed in San Quentin yet."

Don't do it, man. Don't take the first swing.

Whatever Rodriguez had been about to say was cut off when Beth lifted her leg and kicked Rodriquez in the belly. The cowboy's eyes widened then the air in his chest burst from his mouth in a loud grunt and he clutched his midsection.

Mack gaped at Beth when a quiet hush spread through the cowboy ready area.

"I forgot to mention that I'm not only an investment counselor, but I'm a certified kickboxing instructor."

Hot damn. There was a lot more to Beth than he

realized. "You still want to egg me on, Rodriguez?" Mack asked.

The bull rider winced as he straightened up. "No."

Mack escorted Beth farther down the row of chutes, noting the cowboys scrambled out of the way as they passed by. "You were something else back there."

"I hate bullies." She frowned. "What are you smiling at?"

"I've never had a girl stand up for me before."

She dropped her gaze. "Did I embarrass you?"

"Darlin', you didn't embarrass me." He whispered in her ear. "You have no idea how sexy you are…all fired up and ready to rumble." He touched his cheek to hers and felt her shiver. There was nothing friendly about the chemistry between them, and they were fooling nobody by believing they could be friends.

"Mack, is it true that you've gone to jail?"

He wasn't proud of his trips to the slammer. "The charges never stuck."

"When was the last time you took a ride in a squad car?"

"Four years ago when I was twenty-five."

"You're only twenty-nine?"

The surprise in her voice confused him. "How old are you?"

Her chin jutted. "Thirty-one." The line between her eyebrows deepened. "Why didn't the charges ever stick?" she asked.

He set his hand against her lower back and guided her over to a chute where rodeo workers were loading a bronc. He dropped his gear bag, took Beth by the shoulders and looked her in the eye. "The charges didn't stick because I had witnesses who backed up my story. I always try to walk away from a fight, but sometimes the crowd blocks off your escape and you're left with no choice but to fight your way out of a bar." When Beth continued to watch him with wary eyes, he lowered his voice. "You're not afraid of me, are you?"

"No. But I've never known a man who isn't afraid to settle a dispute with his hands."

"Don't tell me your husband never got into a fight."

"Are you kidding?" She snorted. "His face is too valuable to mess up."

What the hell kind of man had Beth married? Any guy who put more stock in his face than his honor was a dweeb.

The announcer introduced the final bareback contestant, which meant Mack had better focus on his own ride and impressing Beth. He removed his saddle from the bag. "I blame my mother. She burdened me with a name that amuses people. After a while the jokes get old."

"I understand." Her soulful brown eyes spoke the truth.

"I'm coming out of this chute. If you stand over there—" he pointed several feet away "—you'll have a better view of the action."

"Sure." She hesitated, shoving her hands into her jeans pockets. The action drew her shirt against her chest, showing the subtle outline of her breasts—breasts that he'd enjoyed.

"Good luck." Beth spun, but Mack caught her arm.

"What about my good-luck kiss?" He held his breath, waiting to see if she'd comply. She didn't disappoint him. She rose on tiptoe but when he attempted to meet her mouth halfway, she turned her head and his kiss landed on her cheek.

"Don't fall off your horse, cowboy."

Mack was as determined to make it to eight as he was to collect a proper kiss from Beth before the day ended.

BETH STOOD IN the shadows watching Mack prepare for his ride—noticing his stony expression and matter-of-fact movements as he put on his spurs and riding glove. If not for his casual glances in her direction she'd almost believe he'd forgotten she existed.

"Ladies and gents, we're ready for the saddle-bronc event!" The announcer's voice thundered over the loudspeaker above her head.

"Folks, in order to score well, the cowboy must spur the whole eight seconds. This event is as close to rodeo ballet as you'll ever get. The cowboy and horse will score highest if they perform together in a smooth, rhythmic ride."

Mack slipped on a protective vest, and Beth breathed a sigh of relief that he wasn't as crazy as some of the cowboys who wore nothing but colorful shirts to protect themselves from a kick to the chest.

"First out of the gate this afternoon is Mack Cash."

The applause that echoed throughout the arena stunned Beth.

The announcer's jovial guffaw added to the noise. *"Sounds as if we have a few Cowboy Rebels fans here today."* A second wave of deafening noise filled the arena. *"For those of you who don't know...Mack Cash is the lead singer of the band Cowboy Rebels."*

"I love you, Mack!" A buckle bunny stood in the stands holding a sign with a pink heart painted on it.

Jealousy pricked Beth. She shoved the stinging sensation aside, but not before she shocked herself by admitting she was jealous of the younger woman. During her short marriage to Brad, never once had she felt envious of women who'd ogled him or stopped him on the street for his autograph.

She had a one-night stand with Mack, and had expected nothing to come of it—so it was crazy that she didn't care for other women lusting after him.

"Cash has his work cut out for him," the announcer said. *"He's drawn Widow Maker and this bucker spins faster than an F-5 tornado!"*

That didn't sound reassuring.

"As with all the events today, for every cowboy who makes it to the buzzer, the First Community Bank is donating a hundred dollars to the medical clinic. Ten cowboys have made the list. Let's see if Cash is gonna be number eleven."

Mack climbed the rails and eased onto the brown-and-white-spotted horse. Beth caught only glimpses of his profile as others gathered close, ready to help him if need be. After the cowboys moved away from the chute, her breath caught in her throat at the magnificent sight Mack made—hat tilted low over his head, his hips and shoulders leaning forward, his mouth pressed into a thin line.

The gate opened and Mack disappeared from view. She rushed closer and climbed the rails, then wished she hadn't when she watched the bronc buck wildly. Mack slid forward in the saddle, and she feared he'd tumble headfirst over the front of the horse, but he managed to hang on—a miracle that was short-lived. Widow Maker vaulted into the air then rotated into a dizzying spin that must have put a horrible strain on Mack's arm. She was amazed the limb didn't tear away from its socket.

How many seconds had passed? She was afraid to take her eyes off Mack. Finally, the buzzer sounded and she breathed a sigh of relief, which she inhaled back into her body when Mack slid down the horse's side. Why didn't he let go? Why was he fighting to stay on the bronc?

The pickup men raced toward the horse, one waving his hands, the other trying to inch close enough to loosen the strap beneath the animal's belly. It happened simultaneously—the flank strap broke free and Mack hit the ground. When he attempted to get to his feet, Widow Maker's hoof caught him in the shoulder and sent him sprawling into the dirt again, while a rodeo helper escorted the horse away.

Beth's heart thudded painfully in her chest as Mack slowly crawled to his feet and collected his battered hat.

"Mack Cash is gonna live to sing another song! Looks like Cash not only earned the clinic an extra hundred dollars, but his score of eighty-one moves him into second place!" The crowd's applause thundered through the stands.

Mack walked gingerly out of the arena, and Beth didn't know what to do. Should she wait where she was or run to him and see if he was okay?

Stay right where you are. You're just friends.

Are you crazy, girl? Go!

As soon as she caught a glimpse of Mack's hat, Beth took off—she couldn't have stopped her legs from moving if she'd tried.

The cowboys congratulating Mack noticed her and stepped aside, then it was just the two of them. In that brief instant she felt protective and possessive of him all at once. She didn't understand her feelings—and didn't care. She needed to know that he was okay and the only way to do that was to touch him.

She launched herself at his chest and squeezed his neck. "Are you hurt?" The scent of dust and sweat and Mack's aftershave enveloped her in a warm hug.

"I'm fine, darlin'."

Beth pressed her lips to Mack's, cheers and whistles echoing in her ears as raw emotion pumped through her veins. Fear for Mack's safety and relief that he was okay gave way to a painful arousal that caught her off guard.

He deepened the kiss, sweeping his tongue inside her mouth. Good thing he held her because her insides had turned to mush, and the only thing preventing her from pulling him to the ground was the fifty or more cowboys watching them.

Mack broke off the kiss, his grin fueling her desire. "If this is the reward waiting for me after my ride, I think I'll retire my guitar and go back on the circuit."

Chapter Five

"Hey, Mack! It's karaoke night at The Barn. You gonna be there?"

Mack stopped walking but didn't release Beth's hand. After the kiss she'd planted on him in front of his competitors, he wasn't letting her out of his sight. "I don't know." He glanced at Beth. "You up for a little dancing after the rodeo?"

"No, thank you. I need to get back to the ranch."

He wanted to ask what for but held his tongue.

"Besides, I'm not dressed for a night on the town."

She was making excuses. "There's nothing wrong with what you're wearing."

"Jeans and a T-shirt with Black Jack Mountain written across the front are hardly dancing attire."

Mack whispered in her ear. "Darlin', it wasn't your clothes that attracted me to you at the Number 10."

She scrunched her nose before admitting, "I would like to hear you sing again."

Yes! He executed a mental fist pump. "Let's grab a bite to eat before we head over to the dance hall." Their dinner took less than an hour and when Mack pulled into the lot behind the bar, which had once been a hay barn, Beth was already squirming in her seat.

"The Barn has a mechanical bull." He grinned. "Saturday is ladies' night. You ride for free."

"Oh, no." She got out of the truck and shut the door before he made it past the hood. "You're not coaxing me onto a bull, Merle Haggard."

"I'm gonna give you a pass on using my given name." He leaned in close and whispered in her ear. "Because it sounds sexy coming from your mouth." He kissed her—a light brush of his lips across hers. When they reached the door, he paid the cover charge then an onslaught of whistles and shouts greeted him as they stepped inside. Beth tensed, and he gave her hand a reassuring squeeze as he led her through the crowd.

"You singing a few Haggard tunes tonight, Mack?" a cowboy at the bar asked.

"You bet I am." He tipped his hat to a group of ladies shouting song titles at him.

He stopped at a table next to the stage. "How's this?"

"Fine." Beth sat with her back to the wall.

"Red wine?" At her nod, he said, "Be right back."

Ten minutes later he set their drinks on the table and took his seat. Beth gulped the wine in her glass, her attention centered on the mechanical bull. Maybe she was drinking up the courage to ride.

"Ladies and gents, welcome to The Barn!" The MC adjusted the microphone stand on the stage. "I'm Mike, your host for the evening." He waited for the clapping to die down. "Saturday night is ladies' night and Todd over there is warming up Rex, our mechanical bull." Todd flipped the switch and the bucking machine spun in quick circles. The buckle bunnies whistled and cheered, then Todd adjusted the speed and the headless bull settled into a slow, rocking motion, drawing catcalls from the cowboys.

"We're running the karaoke contest simultaneously with the cowgirl bull-riding contest," the MC said. "You ladies can listen to your favorite wailing cowboys while you ride!"

The MC waved. "C'mon up on stage, Mack. You know the ladies are waiting for you to sing." Cheers filled the bar. "Mack Cash, the lead singer of the Cowboy Rebels, will go first then we'll see how the rest of you howlers out there measure up."

Mack grabbed Beth's hand. "You ready?"

"Ready for what?"

"The cowboy who comes up on stage to sing gets to pick the girl he wants to ride Rex."

Her eyes widened. "I can't ride that…that…thing." She slid down in her chair.

"I guess I can ask one of the other ladies…" He made a pretense of searching the crowd.

Beth tracked his gaze around the room.

Mack stood and held out his hand. "Honey, there's nothing to it." When she didn't budge, he leaned over the table. "If you can ride me, you can ride that bull." Her cheeks turned red, and he loved that he could make her blush.

"Pick me, Mack! Pick me!" a redhead shouted from across the room.

Beth sprang from her seat. "I'll ride."

Thrilled that she was jealous of the buckle bunny, he tugged her after him.

"Mack Cash has picked his filly." The MC patted the microphone, making loud thumping noises. "What's your name, pretty lady?"

"Beth," Mack shouted.

"Let's see if cowgirl Beth can ride Rex until Mack finishes his song. If she does, then her drinks are on the house tonight!"

Todd helped Beth climb onto the mechanical bull while Mack detoured and took the microphone from the MC. "I'm singing 'Ever Changing Woman' by Merle Haggard." Mack waited for Todd to start the machine. When the bull began moving, Mack belted out the song. He did fine with the first two verses then stumbled when Rex switched directions and Beth began to slide. Todd slowed the machine's movements so Beth could regain her balance. When she sat upright, her body undulated in a way that made him think of soft mattresses and sweet-smelling sheets.

Wolf whistles echoed through the air and Mack's gaze shifted to the rowdy cowboys gathering near Rex. Even though Beth wasn't dressed like a buckle bunny, her T-shirt pulled tight across her chest, revealing the shape and size of her breasts.

Mack forgot about the women in front of the stage ogling him and focused on Beth and the cowboys cheering for her. A possessive heat filled him and when he finished his song, he made a beeline for the bull.

"Cowgirl Beth rode Rex until Mack Cash finished his song." The MC thumped his fingers against the microphone. "Give the lovebirds a round of applause." While the next singing cowboy and lady bull rider were introduced, Mack watched Todd help Beth off the machine. When her feet hit the mat, she pitched forward and Todd caught her by the waist. Their feet tangled and they tumbled to the pad, Beth sprawling on top of Todd. Mack reacted before thinking and swooped in, picking

Beth up and swinging her into his arms. He carried her off the mats and set her on her feet outside the pen.

"I did—"

Whatever Beth had been about to say was cut off by Mack's mouth. When he pulled back, Beth resumed talking as if she'd barely been aware he'd kissed her. "I was pretty good, wasn't I?"

"You rode that bull like a bona fide cowgirl." He ushered her to their table and a waitress placed a glass of red wine in front of her.

"I didn't think I'd like that." She struggled to catch her breath. "It was a lot of fun."

"You're a natural." Maybe he should suggest they leave before she decided she wanted a second go 'round on Rex.

"Excuse me." A deep voice floated over Mack's shoulder. He spun in his seat and swallowed a laugh. The cowboy wore brand-new jeans, a knock-off Western belt, a Wrangler shirt from the sale rack at Sheplers and pointy-toed boots.

"What do you want?" Mack ignored the nudge Beth gave his calf beneath the table. So what if he was rude? He didn't appreciate other men homing in on his girl.

The guy removed his hat, revealing a head of curly hair. "Beth, my name is Larry. Would you care to dance?"

"She wouldn't—"

"I'd love to." Beth was out of her chair and in Larry's arms before Mack picked his jaw up off the floor.

The city slicker, masquerading as a cowboy, pulled her close—way too close for a first dance. With Mack's luck, the guy was probably Beth's type—a corporate stuffed shirt. He didn't let them out of his sight—not even when a pretty blonde asked him to dance. He guided the girl across the dance floor toward Beth and Larry. "Care to switch partners?" Mack deposited the blonde in Larry's arms and whisked Beth away.

Beth laughed. "Mack Cash, I think you're jealous."

"Damn right, I'm jealous." He twirled her across the floor, wishing he hadn't suggested karaoke night at The Barn.

"We're just friends, remember?"

"Yeah, well, a guy's got a right to change his mind."

THE DRIVE BACK to the ranch took forever, leaving Beth plenty of time to think about her and Mack and the crazy game of friendship they were playing. Earlier in the night when the svelte redhead had jumped out of her seat, demanding Mack pick her to ride the mechanical bull the burning jealousy that swept through Beth had shocked her.

She was a grown woman not a simpering buckle bunny. It was time to admit she was losing control of the situation between her and Mack. The more she hung out with him, the more she wanted to be with him—and not just as a friend. She couldn't remember the last time Brad had taken her anywhere to have fun. But because of the popularity of the Cowboy Rebels, fun followed Mack wherever he went. A part of Beth yearned to go along for the ride with him and throw caution to the wind. But with her heart still bruised and battered from the divorce she feared that when her time with Mack ended, her heart would be broken clean through.

"You're awfully quiet." Mack smiled at her.

"I'm tired," she lied. "Riding bulls is hard work."

He chuckled. "Dave's got an old bucking machine

hidden away in the storage room at the back of the barn. I could give you lessons if you want."

"Once was enough, thanks." Beth closed her eyes and imagined Mack sitting behind her on the bull, his arms holding her close as their bodies swayed in rhythm to the machine's movements.

"Have you ever been to Stagecoach?"

"No." She'd heard of the small town but had never ventured east of Yuma except to visit Tucson and the trip to Rattlesnake.

"That's my old stomping ground. I thought maybe next week I'd take you out there and show you around."

"What's there to see?"

"Our family pecan farm for one thing."

Mack had mentioned one of his brothers ran the farm during the chuck wagon cookout with Roger Kline and his business associates.

As much as she was intrigued about seeing the property, she wasn't eager to meet Mack's siblings and answer their questions about her relationship with their brother. "I'm not sure what I'm doing," she hedged.

"Check your schedule and let me know."

Aside from Mack showing her a good time today, he'd also helped her realize that she needed to quit focusing on him and make some decisions about her future.

A future without Mack in it.

"WHAT'S GOING ON that I'm out here two weekends in a row helping with trail rides?" Porter asked Mack.

"Hoss thinks Jake fell off the wagon again." Mack nodded to the grooming kit. "Hand me the currycomb."

Porter tossed the rubber device through the air and

Mack caught it with one hand. They'd spent the better half of an hour brushing the horses after bringing them in from the trail.

"I didn't know Jake had a drinking problem," Porter said. "Shoot, he's close to my age, isn't he?"

"Twenty-eight. He'd been sober for a year when Dave hired him last summer."

Porter snapped his fingers. "Is that why he dropped off the rodeo circuit?"

"I'm guessing that was the reason." Mack felt sorry for Jake. The man's drinking problem had already cost him his marriage, and if he didn't get his act together he might lose shared custody of his daughter, too.

"I don't mind pitching in on weekends, but I'm not looking for a permanent job at the dude ranch."

Mack stopped brushing Speckles. "Are you ever going to get serious about your future, Porter?"

"I don't know what you're talking about." Porter scratched Doink's ears. The horse was Porter's favorite—maybe because they were both goof-offs and acted as if they didn't have a care in the world.

"You haven't held down a forty-hour-a-week job in I can't remember how long."

"Since when have you been concerned about what I do and don't do? You and everyone else were off chasing girls and rodeoing when I was little. Where was your concern then?"

Mack opened his mouth to respond then changed his mind. Porter was right. As the youngest brother, he'd gotten overlooked and had often been told to stay behind or get lost. "You should decide what you want to do with your life before you reach thirty."

"Okay, big shot." Porter punched Mack's shoulder.

"You're gonna be thirty this year. What's your game plan?"

"I'm not certain, but—"

"See!" Porter pointed a finger. "You're doing that… black-pot-kettle thing Grandma Ada always said to us."

"You mean the pot calling the kettle black?"

"Yeah, that's it."

Mack set aside the currycomb. "I've been giving the future a lot of thought." Especially since Andy, the band's drummer, had announced he was quitting the Cowboy Rebels at the end of the year. Andy's wife was tired of him being gone every weekend, and she wanted him home with her and the kids. "I like what I do at the dude ranch."

"Can you earn a decent living here if you work full-time?"

"I've talked with Dave about adding a cattle drive to the activities at the ranch."

"What do you know about cattle?"

"More than you," Mack said. "I herded cows at the Triple D for three summers when I was in high school."

"What did Dave say?"

"He's considering it. I figured it would bring in additional income during the summer when cabin rentals decrease."

"Would you work more hours then?" Porter asked.

"Yep."

"What about the band?"

"I'm getting burned out on the music scene." Meeting Beth had confirmed in Mack's mind that he was ready to give up the nightlife and superficial flings with buckle bunnies. Beth made him want more. Something deeper…richer…rewarding. *And permanent.*

"What do you think of that lady who's a guest here?"

Had his brother made a move on Beth? "Why are you asking?"

"I introduced myself to her, but she seemed kind of serious."

The tightness in Mack's chest eased. "She didn't fall for your flattery, eh?"

"Nope. And I put out my best effort." Porter walked Doink into his stall then shut the gate.

"I offered to take her on a horseback ride, but she claimed you'd already been on the trail with her." Porter grinned. "What's going on between you two?"

Mack played dumb. "Nothing."

"When I mentioned your name, her face turned red."

A week had passed since he'd taken Beth to the rodeo, and he'd only caught glimpses of the woman since. He'd gone out of his way to cross paths with her, but it was as if she sensed whenever he was near and found an escape route before he reached her.

"Mack, are you in here?"

He glanced toward the barn entrance. Beth stood in the swath of sunlight streaming through the doors. "Take a break," he said to his brother.

Porter chuckled, and Mack swore he'd throw a punch if his brother didn't get lost. "Holler if you need my help." Porter approached Beth, stopping in front of her.

Mack wished his brother would keep walking.

"If you change your mind about that ride, give me a shout." Porter tapped a finger against the brim of his hat and left the barn.

Mack expected Beth to move closer but her shoes appeared cemented in place. She wrung her hands as he closed the distance between them. When he stopped in front of her, she straightened her shoulders as if ready to do battle. It had been six days since the rodeo—six days of Beth dodging him. Six nights of reliving their rodeo kiss in his dreams.

"What's wrong?"

"I need to talk to you." She glanced toward the storage room.

"We're alone."

Her posture relaxed and she blew out a quiet breath. "I wanted to apologize."

"I can't think of anything you need to apologize for." His remark brought her head up and the shimmer in her eyes socked him in the gut. *Tears?*

"I shouldn't have kissed you at the rodeo."

His lungs froze in the middle of drawing in air. He sure as hell didn't regret the kiss, and he didn't know what to say.

"I got caught up in the excitement and…"

And what?

"My first experience with the whole rodeo thing."

One of the horses kicked their stall and the loud thump startled her. "Let's get out of here." He led Beth from the barn and stopped beneath the shade of a paloverde tree. "What are you afraid of?"

"I'm not afraid." The crack in her voice betrayed her bravado.

Mack brushed the pad of his thumb against her cheek. "I admit we met under *interesting* circumstances, but I thought we'd decided to start over as friends and—"

"That's just it." Beth moved away, and Mack's arm fell to his side. "Friends don't exchange kisses."

Something more than kissing bothered her but she wasn't making it easy for him to guess. Since he'd learned of her divorce, he'd wondered about her feelings for her ex. "Are you still in love with your ex-husband?"

She broke eye contact and rolled the ball of her shoe across a pebble on the ground.

"We've never really talked about him," he said.

"We haven't talked about all your ex-girlfriends, either." She spun on her heels and took the path that led to her cabin.

Mack hurried after her. "I've got nothing to hide. Ask me anything."

"I don't care to know about all the women you've slept with."

"There haven't been as many as you might believe, considering my line of work." For a short woman she sure had a long stride. He picked up the pace. "If we're friends, it shouldn't matter how many women I've been with."

She stopped in front of her cabin and fished a key from her pocket. He took it from her grasp and opened the door for her, then hovered on the stoop.

"You're doing it again."

"Doing what?" he asked.

"Acting like a boyfriend instead of a friend."

"I can't help it if Grandma Ada taught her grandsons manners."

They squared off, and when she attempted to speak he interrupted her. "I want to be friends with you, and I meant it. I like you, Beth. You're different from other women I've known." She looked everywhere but at him. He entered the cabin and grasped her shoulders. "What's really bothering you?" Her eyes watered again. "Can't we see where this...whatever is happening between us leads?"

"It can't lead anywhere," she whispered.

Not the answer he hoped to hear, yet it wasn't a flat-out *no,* either. "I get that you might need time to—"

"I'm over Brad."

Okay, she was over her ex, but he doubted she'd put his betrayal behind her. "I'm a good listener."

She stiffened. "I don't want to talk about my marriage."

He released her and closed the cabin door. "We don't have to talk."

She licked her lips. "This isn't a good idea."

He eyed the trail of moisture left behind by her tongue then flipped the lock on the door. The quiet *click* echoed through the cabin. "What's not a good idea?"

"You and me alone."

He moved forward.

She retreated. "Don't you have work to do?"

"It'll wait."

Her shallow breathing convinced him that she was as turned on as he was. Why was she fighting her attraction to him? He lowered his head and pressed his lips to hers.

That's all it took—one brush of Mack's lips across Beth's and she lost the will to fight. All she wanted was to be left alone to figure out her next move in life, but Mack was everywhere—always in her thoughts and now here in her cabin. She didn't understand what a man like him saw in her, but he was too handsome, too male, too everything, and she didn't have the strength to resist him.

Trust your instincts.

She trusted that Mack's intentions were honest—he did like her, and there was no denying the attraction between them, but a guy like Mack wasn't looking for forever with a girl like her. She wished with all her heart she hadn't lost her sanity that night at the Number 10 Saloon. Mack had given her a taste of what girls like her could never have. Part of the thrill for him was the chase and once he caught her, he'd grow bored and move on—like Brad had. Heart thudding painfully in her chest, she wrapped her arms around his neck and leaned into him, giving herself over to his expert care.

One kiss turned into two then three and finally he pulled away. "We can take it as slow as you want," he whispered.

The truth was she didn't want to take it slow. She wanted fast. Hard. And often. But if she gave in and lived day by day with Mack, she'd never make plans for the future.

She should leave. Tomorrow. *No, tonight.*

Not yet.

Enjoy Mack while you're at the ranch then move on.

Could she lower her guard and allow them to be friends with benefits, then skip out on him when she found a new job?

"I'm leaving..."

"Stay," he whispered.

"I need to look for a job."

"You're not thinking of searching anywhere else but Yuma, are you?"

"I haven't decided if I want to continue living in the same town as my ex."

"Don't let him run you off."

"If I go, it's because there's nothing to keep me here."

Mack's brown eyes gleamed with intent, and Beth's heart tumbled a little farther down heartache hill.

"Then I guess it's up to me to give you a reason to stay."

Chapter Six

Mack took his promise seriously to change Beth's mind about her feelings for him and remain in Yuma. He couldn't say for sure where their relationship was headed—he only knew he wasn't ready to say goodbye to her. And no matter how she protested, gut instinct insisted that she didn't want to part ways with him—not after the kiss she'd planted on him at the rodeo. He understood her reservation at jumping into a personal relationship so soon after her divorce, but he sensed if he didn't make his move now, he might lose his chance with her.

He blamed Todd at The Barn for the shift in Mack's feelings toward Beth. When Todd had helped her off the bucking machine, leaving his hands on her waist longer than necessary, the green monster attacked Mack. The angsty feeling in his stomach that night had proved his feelings for Beth weren't a passing fancy.

After helping Hoss earlier in the morning, he'd taken the businessmen on their final trail ride. The group had returned to their cabins an hour ago to pack their belongings before the Sunday check-out at noon. Mack went to Dave's office to see if there were any chores needing to be done. If not, he wanted to spend the afternoon with Beth. He entered the main building and rapped his knuckles on the boss's door.

"C'mon in."

"Got a minute?"

Dave sat behind his desk, reading glasses perched on his nose. He held up a sheet of paper. "I've made a decision."

"About adding a cattle drive to the activities at the ranch?" Mack took a seat in the chair across from the desk.

"I made a few calls to local ranchers," Dave said. "They recommend buying the cows from the Still Water Ranch near Bedford."

"Bedford's west of Prescott, isn't it?"

"Yep. Last night I spoke to the owner, Bud Miller. He's got fifty head ready to sell. I want you to drive up there and take a look at the herd before I sign on the dotted line." Dave shuffled a pile of papers scattered across his desk then held up a yellow Post-it note. "The ranch phone number and address." He handed the paper to Mack. "Make sure the animals are in good condition. No pregnant cows and no bulls."

"What about feed for the cattle? Have you found a supplier?"

"The Bar 7 sells hay and they'll deliver to us."

"Do you plan to hire an extra hand to help with the herd?"

Dave's expression sobered. "The only way we're doing this is if you're on the payroll forty hours a week." Dave held up his hand. "I'm willing to try this for one year to see if it attracts more visitors. If it doesn't, I sell the herd. Starting February first, you're eligible for benefits and health insurance."

That was more than Mack expected out of the deal.

"If the herd becomes too much work, especially during the winter months when the ranch is busiest, I'll consider hiring Porter on a permanent part-time basis."

Part-time would suit Porter fine; it was the *permanent* that might scare him off. "When do you want me to go to Bedford?"

"We don't have any guests scheduled until Thursday. You can leave tomorrow."

"You mind if Beth comes with me?" The words were out of his mouth before he realized he'd spoken.

Dave narrowed his eyes. "Are you two dating?"

Keeping a straight face, Mack said, "No. I just thought she might like a break from the ranch for a couple of days."

"You took her to the Rattlesnake Rodeo."

Mack squirmed inside his boots.

Dave glared at Mack. "She's the daughter of a good friend, and I don't need to tell you—"

"Before you say another word, let me assure you that my intentions toward Beth are honorable."

"I know Beth is a grown woman and she's not my daughter, but she's a guest at my ranch and I feel responsible for her."

"I understand."

"You'd better or else…"

His boss didn't need to finish the threat. Mack knew there would be hell to pay or worse—he'd lose his job— if he hurt Beth. Hoping to change the subject, he asked, "Have you heard from Millie?"

"No." Dave reshuffled the stack of papers on the desk. "I hired a new housekeeper. She starts tomorrow."

Mack felt bad that Millie's sudden departure had hurt

his boss. "I'll check in before we leave in the morning." He made a beeline for the barn to give Hoss a heads-up that he'd be gone for a couple of days, but the man was nowhere in sight—probably taking an afternoon nap. Mack stopped at his quarters to shower and change clothes then went in search of Beth. He found her sitting on her cabin porch, staring into the distance. She appeared soft and in need of a hug—his hug. She wore a pink, V-neck T-shirt with jeans—nothing fancy, but sexy all the same.

"How's your day going?" Mack leaned a hip against the porch rail.

"Fine. How about yours?"

"Good. I've got a proposition for you."

She raised an eyebrow.

"Dave's adding a cattle drive to the dude ranch experience and he asked me to check out some livestock in the Prescott Valley. How would you like to tag along with me tomorrow?"

Beth got out of her chair and attempted to pass Mack on her way to the door, but he grasped her arm. He slid his fingers across her flesh, the softness of her skin and the scent of her sultry perfume almost making him forget why he was there. "Say you'll come with me."

"I don't think that's a good idea."

"Why not? The Prescott area is beautiful, and we might even catch a glimpse of snow up there."

"It's tempting, but…" She shook her head. "I need to make a few business calls."

She didn't want to be alone with him. "Business calls? Aren't you taking a hiatus from your job?"

Her teeth worried her lower lip and the innocent action reminded him of when she ran her tongue over the pouty flesh right before he'd kissed her. She pulled free of his grasp. "I don't think we should be alone, Mack."

His ego ballooned at the idea that she viewed him as too much of a temptation. Right then and there he decided he'd do whatever was necessary to make sure she sat next to him in his truck when he drove off tomorrow. "You're free to make business calls while I'm driving." When she remained silent, he said, "I swear nothing will happen that you don't want to happen."

She laughed. "And that's supposed to reassure me?"

"C'mon. Before you know it, your respite at the ranch will be over and you'll be working nine-to-five again." She rubbed her brow and he sensed she was giving his proposition serious consideration.

"When are you leaving?"

The sweet rush of victory swept through him. "After breakfast."

"Okay." She opened the cabin door.

"Bring a warm coat. Never can tell what kind of weather we'll run into north of Phoenix, and don't forget to pack an overnight bag."

"What for?"

"I'd rather wait until the next morning to head back." The last thing he wanted to do was have a tire blow out or hit a deer on a dark road with Beth in the truck.

"Fine." The door shut in his face.

He walked off, grinning.

LATE MONDAY MORNING Beth waited in front of the cantina for Mack to pull up in his truck. Her stomach hadn't stopped fluttering since she'd woken at five. She was both excited and nervous about accompanying him to Prescott.

Since his declaration that he intended to change her mind about him, she'd see-sawed between wanting him to leave her alone and wanting him to fight for her attention, which made her feel even guiltier for accepting his invitation today. A long-term relationship between them wasn't in the picture—at least not the one she painted for them. And she worried he'd accuse her of leading him on when they parted ways.

The sound of a pickup reached her ears seconds before Mack's silver Ford came into view. He put the vehicle in Park, got out and set her overnight bag in the backseat. "You ready?"

No. "Yes."

"Mack!" Dave jogged toward them. "Be careful on the roads today. They're predicting snow near Prescott."

Mack opened Beth's door and she slid onto the seat. "I'll call once I see the herd."

"No need to unless you don't like what you see. Last night I phoned Miller and negotiated a price for the fifty head. All he's waiting for is an okay from you to deliver them to the ranch."

"Sounds good." Mack shut Beth's door and walked around to the driver's side and hopped behind the wheel. "I'm going to make you a promise."

"No more promises." Mack's promises were nothing but trouble.

"Too late." He winked.

He was a big flirt—a flirt Beth was helplessly falling for.

"I promise that you're going to wish the next two days would last forever."

Gathering his words close to her heart she said, "We'll see, cowboy."

He reached across the seat and gently squeezed her fingers. "Yes, ma'am, we will indeed see."

As soon as they reached the highway, Beth announced, "I'm going to close my eyes for a while." Then she promptly fell asleep.

In repose Beth appeared young and innocent, but Mack suspected her husband's betrayal and the subsequent divorce had taken a toll on her. He'd let her sleep, and hopefully she'd be well-rested for a night on the town. Four hours had flown by when Mack took the dirt road that led to the Still Water Ranch.

"We're here already?" Beth yawned and stretched.

"You slept the entire way."

"I'm sorry. I didn't realize how tired I was."

"I'm glad you caught a little shut-eye." He parked in front of the main house then got out and opened Beth's door.

"Howdy!" A man walked toward them.

"You must be Bud."

"That's right."

"I'm Mack Cash." He offered his hand.

"Who's this pretty filly you brought with you?" Bud tipped his hat.

"Beth Richards," she said before Mack could introduce her.

"Welcome to Still Water." Bud pointed to an enclosed pasture. "Those are the cows I handpicked for your boss. Why don't you wander over to the fence and take a look at them while I make a quick phone call."

"Sure thing." Once Bud retreated inside the house, Mack took Beth by the hand and crossed the ranch yard.

"What do you think?" Beth propped her boot on the

lower rail of the fence. A crisp breeze blew her hair across her face and she brushed it aside.

"They look to be in good health. What do you think?" he said.

"Me? I don't know a thing about cattle." Then she motioned to a cow with big white splotches. "That one is pretty."

"She's a beauty, all right." Mack thought Beth was the real beauty. "See how the others are trailing behind her. She's leading them to the grain bin."

"How do you know so much about cattle when you grew up on a pecan farm?"

"I worked summers on a ranch helping my brother Johnny punch cows."

"Not literally, I hope."

He nodded to a steer standing by itself. "That one's a renegade."

"How can you tell?"

"See him stomp the ground."

She nodded.

"He's bored."

"Can you blame him?" She swept an arm in front of her. "There's nothing to do out there but walk around and eat grass."

Beth's comment opened the door to a question he'd wanted to ask her for a while. "Have you always lived in a city?"

"Yes. Why?"

"Did you ever consider living in the country?"

"It's never entered my mind. As far as cities go, Yuma's small compared to San Diego." She eyed the herd. "If I hadn't met Brad and married him, I'd probably be in California right now."

"I guessed you were no Annie Oakley when I met you at the bar."

"I'm the furthest thing from a country girl, but I admit I've enjoyed the peace and quiet at the dude ranch, especially at night when I sit on the porch and watch the sun set."

"You might not be a country girl, but you like to shake things up once in a while."

"Are you going to hold my one night at the Number 10 against me forever?"

Keeping a straight face he said, "You might have more wild oats to sow."

Her expression sobered. "Maybe you're right. I went straight through college and grad school without taking a break. I met and married Brad within a year of starting a new job, and then I worked long hours to prove myself to my employer. I guess I never really let loose."

"Then you need to kick up your heels and party." And Mack wanted to be the man she had a good time with.

"Back to the reason we're here," she said. "What does it matter if that cow is bored?"

"He'll cause trouble in the herd and we need cattle we can trust. A stampede could kill a ranch guest."

"Sounds dangerous. Maybe you should herd sheep, instead."

"That's not even funny."

"What's not funny?" Bud joined them at the fence.

"Beth suggested we herd sheep instead of cows."

"Shame on you, missy. This is cattle country. No sheep allowed."

"So I've been told," she said.

"Sorry about the phone call." Bud took off his cowboy hat and shoved his fingers through his hair.

"I like what I see, except for the lone wolf out there," Mack said.

"He's bored."

Mack sent Beth an I-told-you-so look.

"As long as you drive the cattle once a week and don't let them sit more than a few days in the same spot, he shouldn't cause trouble."

"Okay, then." Mack shook Bud's hand. "You've got yourself a deal."

They settled on a delivery date, then Bud thanked Mack for doing business with the Still Water Ranch and retreated to his office.

"I don't know about you," Mack said, "but I'm starving. Let's grab a bite to eat at the Tepee Truck Stop down the road from here."

"Sure." Beth hopped into the pickup. "Where did you plan to stay the night?" She wondered if he expected her to share a motel room with him. Half of her wanted to fall into Mack's arms again and for one more night pretend she was everything he'd ever wanted or needed, and the other half was afraid it would only lead to heartbreak—hers.

"I thought we'd drive as far as Aguila and check out the Burro Jim Motel."

"The Burro Jim Motel?"

"It's a desert oasis." He laughed. "That's what the website said. There's a big donkey sign in front of the motel."

"I'm not sure I want that kind of fun," she said.

"If we don't like it, there's a Best Western in town."

"That sounds better."

For the second time that day he reached across the seat and grasped her hand. "You've been a good sport. This cattle stuff must be boring as hell."

"Not really." She could get used to Mack reaching for her. Her ex hadn't been a *toucher*—he'd blamed it on his German blood but now she knew better. Brad hadn't been in love with her.

"You'll like the Tepee's Geronimo burger. It's spicy like you."

She snorted. "No one's ever accused me of being spicy." *Only dependable, quiet and polite.*

The drive to the truck stop took twenty-five minutes. When they arrived, the parking lot was crammed with media vehicles and state highway patrol cars.

"Let's find out what happened," Mack said.

Beth didn't unsnap her seat belt.

"What's the matter?"

She swallowed hard, her eyes riveted on the Channel 3 vehicles. No way would she be able to sneak inside the restaurant without running into a reporter. Thank God Brad anchored the sports desk; at least she knew he wouldn't be here. And neither would her old boss, because she'd delivered a baby boy two days ago. Beth had seen the Facebook post. "Let's find a different place to eat."

"And miss out on a Geronimo burger?" He nodded to the trucks. "Aren't you the least bit curious about all this?"

Not really.

Mack got out then skirted the hood and opened her door. As he guided her through the throng of reporters, she focused on her shoes rather than the action in the parking lot.

"Beth? Beth Richards, is that you?"

Mack held up, leaving her no choice but to stop, too. Pasting a fake smile on her face she spoke to the reporter. "Hello, Ramona." Hoping to cut the woman off at the pass, she asked, "What's going on?"

The question took a few seconds to sink into Ramona's head, because the reporter was too busy gawking at Mack. Ramona was four years younger than Beth and with the help of plastic surgeons, the blonde was a knockout. "There's a roadblock a few miles up the highway. A gunman robbed the Savings and Loan in Prescott yesterday, and he was spotted in the area a couple of hours ago. They think he might be holed up in an abandoned cabin near here."

"Is the teller okay?" Beth asked.

Ramona nodded. "The robber got away with two hundred thousand dollars." Ramona's gaze latched on to Mack. "Looks like both you and Brad moved on pretty fast."

"Mack, this is Ramona Simmons. Ramona, this is Mack Cash."

"Nice name. Sounds country music-ish."

Mack flashed his pearly whites. "Nice to meet you."

"We're in a hurry." Beth made a move to step past Ramona but she blocked her escape.

"For what it's worth, I didn't know they'd hooked up until a few months afterward."

Beth's face flamed. This was not a conversation she wanted to have in front of Mack.

"And I'm sorry about the baby. Until Brad told everyone, I had no idea you couldn't—"

"We really need to get going." Beth tugged Mack's arm.

Ramona walked beside them. "Anyway, it looks like you rebounded just fine."

"Good luck with the story." Beth made a dash for the restaurant entrance, Mack's boot heels clunking against the asphalt behind her. A second later his arm came into view when he reached in front of her and opened the door.

She skidded to a halt inside. *Damn.* She squared off with the news anchor. She didn't like the man—not since she'd overheard him joking at the company picnic that Brad was an idiot for marrying her when he could have gotten a woman *way prettier* than she was.

"This is a surprise." The jerk offered his hand to Mack. "Tim Wetzel. Channel 3 news anchor."

"Mack Cash."

Tim glanced between her and Mack. "You two aren't…"

Beth wanted to cry when Mack set his hand against her waist and inched closer. "Aren't what?" he asked.

"I guess I can tell Brad that you're doing a lot better than he thinks." Tim chuckled. "He said you'd gone off the deep end and quit your job."

No way would she stand here and listen to this idiot talk her down. "Good luck with the story." She entered the restaurant and seated herself at a booth next to the windows. Mack slid onto the bench across from her, then a waitress named Peg delivered glasses of water to the table.

"Can I get you anything else to drink while you look over the menus?"

"I'll have coffee, please," Beth said.

"Make that two."

Once Peg left them alone, Beth rubbed a burn mark that marred the Formica tabletop.

"I'm sorry we ran into these folks," Mack said.

"It's not your fault." She peeked up at him. His brown eyes were filled with compassion and questions.

"Beth."

"What?"

"How do all these people know your ex-husband?"

Did you think you could keep Brad's identity a secret forever?

No, but she'd hoped that while she was with Mack she could pretend her ex didn't exist.

"Brad Stevens is…was my husband."

"The sports anchor for Channel 3?"

She nodded.

"He's good. I watch his sportscast every night."

"Apparently, he's good at a lot of things." Like sleeping with her boss.

"What was that woman referring to when she said she'd heard about the baby? What baby is she talking about?"

"Brad got my boss pregnant."

Mack's eyes rounded.

Peg rescued Beth from having to say more when she brought their coffee. "Ready to order?"

"We've changed our minds about eating." Mack left a ten-dollar bill next to his mug then scooted from the booth and offered his hand to Beth. "Let's get out of here."

Clutching his fingers as if they were a lifeline, they left through a side door and made it to the pickup undetected by the news team. A few seconds later, they left the truck stop, the silence in the cab suffocating.

Chapter Seven

Mack gripped the steering wheel, wishing his fingers were squeezing the news anchor's neck. Who did the guy think he was, speaking to Beth that way? Mack had known Beth's husband had cheated on her—but with her boss? That was low. No wonder she'd quit her job.

He glanced across the seat. Beth stared straight ahead—probably not seeing a damn thing out the windshield.

"You can stop worrying," she said.

"About what?"

She looked at him, her pretty brown eyes clouded with pain. "That I'm going to lose it. Fall apart. Become hysterical."

"You did that already?"

"That's what the night at the Number 10 was all about."

He didn't believe her. Beth was an investment adviser. She calculated numbers. A person like her pondered, gathered facts and analyzed data for eons before reaching a conclusion or, in her case, reacting to an event. He'd bet his Gibson guitar that she hadn't yet come to grips with her husband's betrayal.

He wasn't in any position to dole out advice, but

maybe he could take her mind off running into the TV crew. Besides, with the highway blocked indefinitely, the best place to find a decent motel room for the night was in Prescott. "I know where we're going."

"Where?"

"The Bird Cage Saloon." At her frown he asked, "Have you ever heard of the famous Whiskey Row in Prescott?"

"No."

"During the 1800s the street was lined with bars from one end to the other. A fire destroyed the block in 1900 but they rebuilt it exactly, using brick, and it's become a tourist attraction. My band's played at the Bird Cage."

"Why are we going to a bar?"

"Because you need to let loose." He held his breath, wondering if she'd agree to his plan.

"Okay, I'm game."

Relief swept through Mack. Tonight would be a do-over of their first meeting, only it would end differently—he'd wake up in the morning with Beth in his arms.

They reached Prescott at dusk and he parked in front of the saloon. When they entered the Bird Cage a band Mack wasn't familiar with played on stage. He guided Beth to a booth in the corner.

"Mack, it's good to see you."

"Hey, Stella." He motioned to Beth. "This is a friend of mine, Beth Richards. Beth, Stella and her brother Stan own the place."

After the women exchanged greetings, Stella asked, "How come the Cowboy Rebels aren't on our summer schedule?"

"Andy's hanging out with his family more." And after meeting Beth, Mack was certain that he wanted to be with her on his days off from the ranch.

"You're always welcome to drop by and sing a few songs whenever you want." Stella nodded to Beth. "What would you like to drink, honey?"

"Red wine—" She waved a hand in the air. "Make that a margarita, please." She winked at Mack. "You said I need to let loose."

"Frozen or on the rocks?" Stella asked.

"On the rocks."

"Mack?"

"I'll take my usual."

After Stella walked off, Beth asked, "What's your usual?"

"Blue Moon."

"A beer is hardly adventurous."

"Wait until later." He kissed her neck. "I'll show you how adventurous I can be." When he gazed into Beth's eyes, he felt that familiar tug in his gut. Yeah, he was attracted to her and wanted to make love to her, but the pulling sensation inside him wasn't the result of a surge of testosterone. Beth was the first woman he was comfortable...relaxed...content with. He couldn't remember ever feeling like this before.

"Here you go." Stella placed the drinks on the table. "Are you ordering off the menu?"

Beth nudged him in the side with her elbow, breaking the trance Mack had been under. "I'm sorry." He glanced at Stella. "What did you say?"

"That's interesting. I've never seen you this smitten with a woman. Be back in a few minutes to take your order."

"What are you smiling at?" Beth asked.

"Stella's right." He tucked a strand of hair behind her ear. "I'm smitten."

Beth snorted.

He handed her the margarita, then clanked his beer bottle against the rim of her glass. "Here's to wherever this leads." He hoped to heck the journey was a long one, because he was in no hurry to say goodbye to Beth.

"Ooh, this is good!" She swallowed a second gulp.

"Better than your usual?"

"I like red wine. It's healthy for you."

"You're too young to worry about your health."

She drained her margarita glass, and Mack signaled Stella to bring her a second then leaned closer. God, she smelled good. "Have I mentioned I like that you're a couple of years older than me?"

"It's rude to bring up a lady's age."

"That whole wisdom-comes-with-age thing turns me on." He kissed the soft patch of skin below her ear then licked the tiny spot with his tongue. "Older means wiser, better, more experienced—"

"I'm none of those things."

Stella showed up with round two. "Doesn't appear you're ready to order."

"I'll wave you down when we decide," Mack said.

Stella went to talk to the band, who'd taken a break. A quarter found its way into the jukebox and an old Merle Haggard song filled the bar. Mack stood. "Dance with me?"

There it was again—that flicker of doubt in her eyes. After a moment's hesitation she put her hand in his and he led her onto the floor. He pulled her close and held her hand against his heart. They swayed to the music and Beth relaxed in his arms. He hoped it was *him* and not the alcohol lowering her guard.

"Mack?"

He rubbed his cheek against hers. "What?"

"Why do men cheat?"

He held her tighter—wishing he could shield her from hurt. "Men cheat because they're assholes."

Her fingers played with his shirt button. "Are you including yourself in that category?"

"I'm no saint, and I've done a few stupid things in my life that probably made Grandma Ada spin in her grave." He looked Beth in the eye. "But I've never cheated on a woman."

A sigh escaped her mouth, the puff of air buffeting his neck in a gentle caress. The need to kiss her overwhelmed him, and he lowered his head—

"Is that you, Mack Cash?"

Startled, he glanced up. "Steve Bulldog Bennigan." Keeping one hand against Beth's lower back he greeted his former rodeo partner.

Steve eyed Beth. "Hello, darlin'." He glanced at Mack. "I see your taste in women has improved."

"This is Beth Richards. Beth, Steve Bennigan. We traveled the circuit together for a few years."

Steve grasped Beth's hand and kissed her knuckles. She seemed reluctant to pull her hand free from his grip.

The door opened and another cowboy entered the bar. "Hey, Blake." Steve waved the man over. "Look who I ran into."

Blake removed his hat and offered Mack his hand, his eyes straying to Beth. "Ma'am."

"This is Mack's girlfriend, Beth Richards," Steve said.

"Nice to meet you." Blake spoke to Mack. "Are you and the band playing tonight?"

"'Fraid not. Beth and I are here on business."

"You in a hurry or do you have time for a game of poker?" Steve asked.

"Go ahead and play cards with your friends, Mack." Beth smiled. "It's been a long day. I think I'll say good-night."

The hell she would. He snagged her arm before she took a step. "Thanks, guys, but—"

"Beth," Steve said, "do you know how to play poker?"

"Of course."

Mack gaped at her. "You do?"

"My grandfather taught me to play when I visited him at the retirement home."

Well, shoot. What else didn't he know about his *friend?*

"I'm in," she said then walked off to retrieve her margarita glass.

What happened to *It's been a long day?*

"She's not your usual date," Blake said.

Steve landed a playful punch on Mack's shoulder. "She doesn't have big hair, and she doesn't wear hooker makeup or rhinestones."

You should have seen her when we met.

"I like her," Steve said. "And she can play poker. She'll fit right in with your brothers."

Good thing most of his poker-playing brothers were married.

Blake waved at Stella and asked for a deck of cards, then he and Steve ordered beers and they took their seats at a table across from the bar. Once Beth joined them, Steve dealt the first hand.

After a few minutes, Blake said, "I call."

Everyone laid their hands down then Mack gaped at Beth's full house.

"You weren't kidding." Steve spoke to Beth. "You do know how to play."

"If I have my way, gentlemen, you won't go home with any change in your pockets tonight." Beth offered Steve another smile, and Mack tamped down the urge to end the card game. Steve was a nice guy, and it was obvious that Beth found him entertaining.

An hour passed, and the bar grew crowded. Stella delivered a fourth round of drinks. The alcohol had relaxed Beth, and she giggled at Steve's jokes way too much for Mack's liking.

It was Blake's turn to deal and one of the cards flew off the table. When Beth leaned over to pick it up, she lost her balance and the chair slid out from beneath her, propelling her across Steve's lap.

"Well, happy birthday to me!" Steve helped Beth to her feet.

Everyone had had enough to drink. "It's been a long day, Beth. Would you like to leave?"

"Stay," Steve said. "I want a chance to win back my money."

"Actually," Beth said, retrieving her purse from the back of the chair. "I will call it a night."

"It was fun catching up with you guys." Mack waved at Stella. "I'll settle my tab tomorrow before we leave town." Taking Beth's hand, he led her out of the bar and into the cool night air. "Let's see if the St. Michael has a room."

The historic hotel sat at the end of the block across from the courthouse park. The lobby was empty when they entered, save for the young girl standing behind the check-in desk.

"May I help you?"

"We'd like a room." Mack pulled his wallet from his pocket and removed a credit card.

"How many nights?"

"Just one."

Beth rapped her knuckles on the counter. "Two beds." She winked at Mack. "I don't want to take advantage of you."

Beth must be tipsier than he'd thought. The desk clerk's mouth quivered as she entered the credit information into the computer then handed Mack a pair of key cards. "Your room is on the second floor."

They took the elevator ride in silence. After he let Beth into the room, he said, "Lock the door after me."

"Why?"

"I'm going to move the pickup to the hotel parking lot and get our bags."

"Mack."

"What?"

"I mean it. I'm not going to take advantage of you."

Their gazes clashed and he wished he could figure out what message her dark eyes were sending him. "I know." He left, wondering if he had a chance in hell of salvaging the night.

YOU'RE AN IDIOT.

Beth sat on the bed in the hotel room. She had no idea what had gotten into her tonight—flirting with Mack's friends during the poker game. Both Steve and

Blake were great guys and yes their interest in her—especially Steve's—had soothed her battered ego. Steve was an average-looking guy and since she was an average-looking girl, it was easier to believe his flattery was more sincere than Mack's. There was still a part of Beth that feared Mack saw her as a challenge. Like her ex, Mack was handsome enough to get any woman he wanted. Why he'd set his sights on her was a mystery.

Her growling stomach propelled her off the bed. She perused the room-service menu then ordered steaks, baked potatoes and broccoli for both her and Mack. Forgetting that she didn't have her overnight bag, she retreated to the bathroom and took a shower. She stood beneath the hot spray, hoping the warm steam would clear her head.

She'd told Mack nothing was going to happen between them tonight, yet she yearned to make love with him and pretend for a few hours that they were a perfect match. But she knew in her heart she wasn't the right woman for him, and it was only a matter of time before he came to the same conclusion.

The bathroom door creaked open and she froze. Would he try to join her in the shower? She held her breath, waiting for his hand to pull back the curtain. Instead, the door closed, and disappointment sent a cold shiver through her. She shut off the shower, dried herself then stepped from the tub and spotted her overnight bag on the floor. Why did Mack have to be so thoughtful?

She dressed in her lounge pants and long-sleeve cotton shirt then applied a dab of moisturizer to her face and neck before pinning up her wet hair with a clip. She checked her image in the mirror and couldn't remember what the Beth at the Number 10 Saloon looked like anymore. When she left the bathroom, she found Mack pacing in front of the window. "What's the matter?"

"Nothing." He frowned at her outfit. "I thought we'd go out for a bite to eat."

"I ordered room service. I hope you don't mind." As if on cue, a knock sounded.

"I'll get it." Mack opened the door. A young man wheeled the cart inside and the scent of grilled steak wafted through the air. "Thank you." Mack handed the waiter a tip then locked up behind him.

Beth cleared the travel brochures off the table and Mack pushed the cart closer. "Smells good," he said.

Together they set out the food then sat down. Neither spoke. Surprisingly, the steak was better than Beth expected—or maybe she was so hungry anything would taste good. Mack on the other hand toyed with his meat.

"Is it too well-done?"

"No." He pushed his broccoli into a pile.

"You don't like broccoli?"

He stabbed his fork into the foil-wrapped potato then scooted his chair back and stood. "You want to know what's wrong?"

She set her utensil down.

"There." He pointed his finger at her.

"There what?"

"Your attitude."

She gaped. "My attitude?"

"The way you're acting right now."

"I don't understand."

"When we're together, you're formal, polite and re-served. But tonight playing cards with Steve and Blake you were—" he waved his arm in the air "—funny, sweet and charming. You joked and laughed with them." Mack's pupils grew until his brown eyes appeared black.

There had been one other instance when Beth had witnessed his eyes change color—at the El Rancho Motel when he'd tumbled her to the bed, then… She'd forgotten she was holding her breath and gasped with the sudden need for oxygen.

"You're jealous," she whispered, awed that Mack was envious of his friends—guys who couldn't hold a candle to his good looks, sexy body and cowboy charm.

His chin jutted as if he wanted to deny her charge. Wanted her to believe he was as confident as his reputation portrayed him to be. Then his shoulders slumped, and she lost a tiny piece of her heart to him.

"You're the first, you know," he said.

"First what?"

"First woman who's ever made me feel jealous of another guy."

If her heart wasn't swooning inside her chest she might have laughed at his admission. "I'm not interested in Steve or Blake."

"You smiled more at Steve than you've smiled at me since we've known each other." Mack sucked in a deep breath. "*I* want to be the reason you smile more." He poked his finger in his chest. "*I* want to make you laugh and act relaxed with me." His eyes shone with sincerity, and it was all Beth could do not to launch herself at him and hug him until he stopped looking so sad.

"I can't be that way with you, Mack."

"Why not?" he asked, his voice hoarse.

Dear God. It really mattered to him. *She* really mattered to him. "Because." There would be no going back once she told the truth. She willed her conscience to talk sense into her before she chose a path she couldn't retreat from, but the voice in her head remained silent. She left her chair and approached him.

"I can't laugh or joke or be natural with you because—" she trailed her fingertips across the whiskers covering his cheeks, his chin, down his neck to the beating pulse at the base of his throat "—all I think about when I'm with you is doing this." Rising on tiptoe she pressed her lips to Mack's. His groan rumbled into her mouth and reverberated through her body.

Chapter Eight

Mack froze, the muscles in his body turning to stone as Beth pressed herself against him and deepened the kiss. The tip of her tongue asked for entrance into his mouth and he obliged. Her fingers tangled in his hair, nails scraping across his scalp, sending shivers down his spine.

She had to know she was driving him crazy. He grasped her hips and thrust his hardness against her as she popped the snaps open on his shirt.

"I'm growing fond of Western shirts." Her lips nuzzled his nipple and he groaned. "Easier access to a man's chest."

A man's chest... He wished to hell she'd stop speaking in general terms. He worried that Beth only saw him as a temporary amusement—her rebound guy like the female reporter insinuated earlier in the day at the truck stop. Going their separate ways was not what Mack imagined when he was with Beth.

"As much as I like your shirt," she said, "I'd rather see it on the floor." She tugged the material down his arms and over his wrists. Her hands hovered in front of his belt.

C'mon, darlin'. Don't chicken out on me.

She grasped the buckle, but instead of pulling the belt free her finger traced the etching in the metal—a cowboy wrestling a steer. "Is this real?"

That she thought he might wear a fake championship buckle stung. "It's real."

"Most men with big egos exaggerate their accomplishments."

Why did he get the feeling she was comparing him to her ex? "I won the buckle at a rodeo in Amarillo when I was twenty-three."

She pulled the belt through the jean loops and let it fall to the floor. When she hesitated, he teased, "Aren't you going to finish the job?"

There was a hint of uncertainty in her eyes before she reached for his zipper. She tugged slowly until his boxers were visible. Then she smiled.

"What?"

"I'm surprised by the underwear."

The night at the El Rancho Motel, Beth had disrobed in the bathroom and when she'd come out, he'd already been lying in bed naked waiting for her. "What were you expecting—nothing at all?"

"Maybe."

There it was again—that note of confusion in her voice. "Why nothing?"

"Because it fits your playboy image."

Playboy image? Mack wanted to ask if her ex had gone naked under his slacks, but decided he didn't want to know. "When are you taking off your clothes?"

She grabbed the hem of her long-sleeve T-shirt and lifted it over her head. "There. Now we're both bare-chested." She thrust her breasts out, begging him to touch her.

This didn't feel right. Beth's boldness was new—different from the night at the El Rancho, and the shadow of desperation in her eyes made him nervous. He didn't want her making love with him just because they were sharing a motel room. "It's been a long day," he said. And an emotional one for Beth. "If you'd rather—"

She rubbed her finger across his lips, halting his words. When her breasts flattened against his chest, the contact sizzled and he lost his train of thought. *Oh, hell.* He scooped her into his arms and deposited her in the middle of the bed before hitting the light switch. A crack in the curtains allowed a sliver of light from the streetlamp to illuminate the room. Tonight he wanted to see Beth's face when he melted into her body.

First things first. "What about your dinner?"

"The only thing I'm hungry for is you." She patted the mattress. "Come to bed, Mack."

"Do you mind if I finish the job you started?" His hands paused at the waistband of his jeans.

She flashed a shy smile—this was the Beth he wanted to make love to. As much as he enjoyed her brazenness and flirting, the woman he yearned for was the real Beth, not the rhinestone-covered beauty. He shoved his jeans over his hips, the boxers going along for the ride, then he stretched out next to her.

He wanted this to be perfect—like he'd imagined in his dreams. He snuck his fingers beneath the waistband of her pants and tugged them down her legs, tossing them on top of his jeans on the floor. He began at her ankles, running his fingers up her calves, over her thighs and across her hips then against the little ridges along her spine.

She squirmed, enticing him closer. He wanted to

go slow but the muscles in his body burned with a desperate need to take her fast and hard. He inhaled deeply, hoping to slow the surge of testosterone pumping through his bloodstream, but her sweet, feminine scent went to his head, and he pulled her beneath him. Bracing himself on his elbows he gazed into her eyes. "Tell me now if you want to slow things down."

"Do you want to go slower?"

"Not on your life, but I will if—"

"Then don't," she whispered.

He tangled a hand in her hair and spread kisses across her face, along her neck, over her breasts and stomach. And she didn't protest when his mouth roamed down the rest of her body.

Mack lost himself in Beth and their lovemaking, focusing all his energy on bringing her pleasure. He'd managed to maintain control until she reversed their positions and embarked on her own journey, exploring his body with abandon. When he reached his limit, he fumbled for his jeans. After he removed a condom from his wallet, Beth straddled his waist.

"This is as close to a real cowgirl as I'm ever going to be.... Let's ride."

And ride they did. When Beth collapsed on top of him, he held her close, awed and amazed by what they'd shared. His heart swelled when he felt her brush a kiss against his biceps then squeeze the muscle as if she never wanted to let go of him. When the sound of her even breathing reached his ear, Mack allowed himself to relax.

He'd gotten his wish tonight. Beth had fallen asleep in his arms.

BETH WOKE COCOONED in Mack's warmth, their bodies entwined on the mattress. The clock on the nightstand read 3:30 a.m. She closed her eyes and listened to his breathing. His steady heartbeat beneath her ear almost made her believe last night was the beginning of forever with him.

Good Lord, what had she done?

Flashbacks of their lovemaking—his tenderness and her boldness—filled her head, and her heart beat faster until she worried she'd suffer an anxiety attack. What kind of game was she playing? Brad had landed a blow that had sent her to her knees when he'd admitted he'd only married her to further his career. How was the way she carried on with Mack much different?

A lump formed in her throat. Mack made her feel alive. He made her feel worthy. Desirable. His attraction to her had restored her self-confidence. In his arms she could almost believe he was her soul mate.

She lifted herself off him and studied his handsome face relaxed in sleep. When she stroked the prickly stubble along his jaw, her heart filled with tenderness. She couldn't remember feeling this way about Brad.

Give Mack a chance.

Everything inside Beth yearned to allow Mack closer. To trust him. To believe he wouldn't abandon her when he found out she couldn't have children. Making love with him had only confirmed her worst fear— she'd never survive losing him if she gave him her heart. Then down the road he decided he wanted the family that she couldn't give him.

"What are you staring at?" His whispered words startled her.

She brushed her fingertip over his closed eyelids.

"You're sleeping. How did you know I was watching you?"

"I can feel you." His arm tightened against her. "Just say the word and I'm all yours again."

Shoving her cares aside, she whispered, "Word."

He flipped their positions and nibbled her neck until she giggled. The warm tenderness she'd felt only moments ago quickly heated to a boil and spread through her body. His mouth caught hers in a deep, wet kiss that made her crave his touch. "I want you…now."

And to make sure he understood her urgency she poured her heart and soul into kissing him, leaving nothing of herself behind.

MACK CRACKED AN EYELID open and spotted Beth's head resting on his heart. Last night had ended better than he'd hoped. Beth had finally let herself go in his arms. Unlike the first time they'd been together, she'd held nothing back in her lovemaking, and he believed they'd taken a huge step forward in their relationship.

They hadn't just made love—they'd connected on a deeper level—a place he hadn't gone with any other woman and he felt confident that they were building a relationship with depth, substance and longevity.

"Are you awake?" Her breath caressed his nipple and he shuddered.

"How'd you sleep?" he asked.

She offered him a lazy smile. "I can't remember sleeping."

"Don't blame me if you're tired. You were insatiable."

She gasped. "No—you couldn't get enough of me."

He flipped her onto her back. "You're right. I can't

get enough of you." He kissed her long and slow with a hint of tongue. When he pulled back, she wouldn't make eye contact, and his blood chilled. "What's wrong?"

"Nothing." She glanced at the clock. "We'd better get going."

He hugged her close, wanting to tell her about the dream he'd had—him and her raising a handful of kids, two dogs and a cat in a house with a huge fenced yard, a patio with a built-in grill and an extra-long picnic table so the whole family could eat together. Before he had a chance to speak, Beth retreated to the bathroom. He reached for the TV remote, wanting to check the weather while he waited for his turn in the shower. Thirty minutes later Beth vacated the bathroom, wearing jeans and a pink cotton blouse.

"It's all yours," she said. "I'm going to check out the free breakfast buffet."

"Beth."

She stopped at the door, but kept her back to him.

"Are you okay?"

"Sure."

"No regrets?"

"None." Her voice wobbled and Mack's gut tightened.

"Then why won't you look me in the eye?"

She peeked over her shoulder. "You're naked."

He grinned. "You liked my nakedness last night."

"Yes, but your magnificent nakedness was in bed." She left, forgetting to take a key card with her.

Mack hurried through his shower, and dressed. While he waited for Beth to return, he opened the curtains and stared at the street below. When a knock sounded at the door, he came face-to-face with a banana.

"I thought you might be hungry." Beth inched past him then placed the fruit on the table. "Ready to check out?"

"Not yet."

She took a deep breath as if bracing herself for an argument.

"Why do I get the feeling you're fighting us being a couple?"

"We're not…a couple."

"Then what are we?"

She drew circles on the table with her finger. "Do we have to put a label on our time together?"

Okay, he could live with that. Her divorce was still raw. She might need to grow accustomed to being in a relationship again. "Will you tell me one thing?"

"What?"

"Why did you let your guard down with Steve and Blake?" *But you don't with me?*

"Because Steve and Blake are just like me."

"What's that supposed to mean?"

"I don't have to pretend I'm something I'm not with those guys. They're nice, average men."

"Are you saying that when you're with me you're acting?"

"C'mon, Mack. Look at me." She tugged on the hem of her blouse.

"I am looking at you."

"Really look at me. I'm nothing special. Girls like me are better off with the Steves and Blakes of the world. We don't have to pretend to be better, prettier or more exciting."

"So you believe a girl like you wouldn't be interested

in more than an affair with a guy like me because you assume I'll eventually tire of you and move on?"

She opened her mouth to answer but nothing came out.

Anger simmered in his gut and he viewed his good looks and rock-star reputation as a curse—a first for him. "I wish you'd stop comparing me to your ex-husband."

She crossed the room and stood in front of the window. "Brad used me to further his career. His agent convinced him that the TV station would look more favorably upon him if he was settled with a nice, down-to-earth wife. When he saw me, he thought I was perfect for the role. A few months after we married, he got promoted to sports anchor."

"I don't have an agent and my boss couldn't care less who I date." Well, maybe that wasn't exactly the truth—Dave had warned him not to hurt Beth.

"Guys like you and Brad, the ones who were blessed with exceptional looks and popularity, can have any woman you want."

There she went again bringing up his looks. He was pleased she found him attractive, but he wished she'd see that he was more than a handsome face. He'd never met such a stubborn woman in his life, yet he sensed if he pushed her too far he'd get nowhere. Beth responded better to action than to words. He'd have to show her he was more than a fun roll in the hay. The problem was keeping her with him long enough to accomplish the task.

Right then his cell phone went off. He glanced at the number. "I have to get this." He accepted the call then said, "What's up, Conway?" He tried to ignore

Beth's troubled expression and focus on his brother's panicked voice.

"Isi's having a C-section this afternoon."

"I thought she was going into the hospital next week to have the girls?"

"She was. The doctor's grandfather died and he's leaving town tomorrow," Conway said. "He offered to do the C-section today and Isi's adamant that she wants him and no other doctor. We're heading to the hospital now but Isi's friend, who was going to watch the boys, can't take them today because she's sick, and you're the first person in the family who answered their phone. I need you to be at the farm when the boys get home from school at three-thirty." His brother spoke in a hurry—the father-to-be had been caught off guard by the change in plans and was a nervous wreck.

Mack checked his watch. "I'll be there to meet the boys' bus."

"Thanks, Mack."

Before he had a chance to wish Conway and Isi good luck in the delivery room, his brother hung up.

"What's happened?" Beth asked.

"We need to hit the road. My sister-in-law is having a C-section today and delivering the twins."

Beth grabbed her overnight bag.

He held the door open for her and they left the room. Good thing he'd prepaid the hotel bill last night. He nodded to the desk clerk on their way out the door. As soon as he'd loaded their luggage into the truck, he said, "Be right back. I need to settle my tab with Stella."

He jogged across the street and entered the Bird Cage. Stella was off but the waitress on duty took Mack's credit card. After he signed the receipt and returned to the truck, they drove out of town. Once they cleared the city limits, he put the pedal to the metal, easing up when the speedometer reached eighty. Five miles over the speed limit shouldn't alert any highway deputies.

"Is this an emergency C-section?" Beth asked.

"Isi was scheduled to go into the hospital next week but her doctor had a family emergency, so she decided to deliver the girls today." Mack could feel Beth's eyes on him as he drove.

"What does your brother want you to do?"

"Take care of the twins after school." He glanced across the seat. "I won't be able to drop you off at the dude ranch before the bus arrives at the farm."

"That's okay."

She didn't sound like it was okay. "I can drive you out to the ranch after we get the boys."

"Whatever works best," she said.

Exactly what he didn't want to hear. Mack shoved his worries about Beth aside. His family needed him.

And family trumped his love life.

Chapter Nine

"The bus should be here any minute." Mack tapped his fingers against the steering wheel. They'd arrived at the pecan farm with minutes to spare before the bus dropped off the twins.

"Are you nervous about taking care of the boys?" Beth asked.

"No, why?"

She nodded to his fidgety fingers.

"Sorry." He set his hands on his thighs. "They're good kids."

She hadn't interacted with any children since she'd babysat as a teenager. At sixteen, she got a job at a clothing store in the mall and quit babysitting. Later in life when her friends began having families, she declined invites to barbecues and Christmas parties if their little ones were going to be present. Even though she'd made peace with her sterility, children were a sad reminder of what she'd never experience.

"Are the boys difficult to tell apart?" she asked.

"I had trouble figuring out who was who until I got to know them better. Miguel is the talkative one. He's always on the move. Javier is quiet. He hangs back and watches people."

"You said they were in kindergarten."

"Different teachers. Conway and Isi thought it would be best to separate them so they had a chance to make their own friends."

"Are they happy in separate classrooms?"

"Miguel doesn't mind, but Conway said Javi misses his brother. In preschool, Javi got picked on because of his shyness, and Miguel always had his back. Now Javi has to stand up for himself."

"I hate bullies."

"Were you teased in school?"

"The entire year of sixth grade."

"Why?"

"I was chubby. When all the other girls were developing breasts, I was growing a muffin top." Beth's hormones had gone haywire, and it wasn't until the beginning of seventh grade that doctors figured out why and diagnosed her with polycystic ovary syndrome. They'd put her on medication but she'd still experienced painful periods that had landed her in the ER, so the doctors determined it was best to remove her ovaries.

Mack pointed out the windshield. "Here they come."

She held her breath and fumbled for the door handle.

"Wait in the truck," he said. "It'll only take a second to get them."

Glad for the reprieve, she watched the bus come to a stop. The door opened and Mack exchanged a few words with the driver, then the boys got off with their backpacks. They wore matching shirts in different colors—one blue, one red. Both had jeans on and the same athletic shoes. They had dark brown hair—one neatly styled, the other messy as if he'd walked in front of a wind machine. The messy-haired kid's shirt was untucked and his shoelaces untied. The other boy's clothes were neat and tidy. If she had to guess—Javier was the well-groomed brother and Miguel the rumpled one.

Instead of ushering them to the pickup, Mack listened while both boys spoke at once. His gaze swung between the twins, and she wished she could hear the conversation. Then Miguel looked at her, his eyes assessing. When Javier noticed her, he leaned against his uncle's leg. Mack waved as the bus pulled onto the road and drove off, then he led the boys to the truck and helped them into the backseat.

When Mack got behind the wheel, he made the introductions. "Guys, this is a friend of mine, Beth Richards. Beth, this is Javier and Miguel."

"Nice to meet you, boys." Beth reached over the seat and offered her hand first to Javier. He tentatively grasped her fingers before she switched to Miguel, who squeezed her hand hard and said, "How come you're Uncle Mack's friend?"

"Your uncle and I met at the dude ranch."

"Do you like to go on trail rides?" Miguel asked.

"Not so much. I'd rather sit on my cabin porch and relax."

"That sucks."

"Miguel, your dad told you not to use that word anymore," Mack said.

"Dad's not here."

Javier shoved his brother's shoulder. "You're gonna be in trouble."

Beth covered her smile behind a cough.

"You say *suck,* too," Miguel said.

"No, I don't."

"Yes, you do."

"Okay, that's enough. No fighting in front of Beth."

"Uncle Mack." Javier spoke as the truck pulled into the yard.

"What?"

"I'm hungry."

"Then, let's eat." Mack shut off the engine and helped the boys from the backseat.

Beth studied the farmhouse. The two-story home appeared as if it had recently received a fresh coat of white paint. Toys were strewn across the porch and a pair of bicycles sat in the yard. A *woof* echoed through the air.

"Can Bandit come inside?" Javier asked.

"Sure." Mack chuckled as the twins raced across the grass to unchain their pal. The Lab jumped on the boys, teasing giggles from them. Then the dog went up on hind legs and rested his big paws on Miguel's shoulders.

"Look, Uncle Mack! Bandit wants to dance."

Beth couldn't help but laugh at the trio's antics. "I assume the boys and Bandit are inseparable."

"Yeah. The second day Mig and Javi left for school, the dog chased the bus for two miles before the driver spotted him and pulled off the road."

Beth envisioned the black Lab running down the highway. "What happened?"

"The driver let the dog onto the bus. The school called and Conway had to go into town and pick him up. After that incident, they had to chain Bandit to his doghouse during the day." Mack took her hand and led her across the driveway. The boys and Bandit beat them to the porch.

When Mack opened the door, Beth asked, "Don't they lock the house when they leave?"

"They usually do. Conway must have forgotten. I

bet my brother was so nervous he made Isi drive them to the hospital."

When they entered the kitchen the boys were already seated at the table, Bandit panting by their side. Mack rummaged through the shelves in the pantry. "What do you guys eat after school?" He tossed a package of cookies on the table, then a box of Cheerios and a plastic container of crackers.

The twins dove into the treats and before Beth realized she'd spoken, the words were out of her mouth. "Shouldn't you wash your hands first?"

The boys stopped chewing, their cheeks puffed out like chipmunks. They looked at Mack.

"Beth's right. Wash your hands." He nodded to the doorway and the boys shoved their chairs back and left the room, Bandit by their sides. They didn't go far. She saw them duck through a doorway in the hall and then heard running water.

"Can I get you anything?" Mack opened the fridge and peered inside.

"No, thanks. I'm fine."

"I want milk." Miguel marched into the kitchen. He looked at Beth. "Please."

"Me, too, Uncle Mack." Javier slid onto his chair. "Please."

While Mack poured the milk, Beth spoke to the boys. "I can tell you're both really smart."

"How?" Miguel asked.

"Because smart people always use their manners."

Javier reached for a cracker. "My mom makes me say please but my dad forgets."

"She's my mom, too," Miguel said.

"And you both will have to share your mom with your sisters." Mack ruffled the boys' hair.

"Did Uncle Mack tell you our mom's gonna have two babies?" Javier asked.

Beth took a seat at the table, finding herself drawn to Mack's nephews, which was unusual because she had no practice conversing with kids. "Yes, he did. Do you think your sisters will look alike?"

Javier nodded and Miguel said, "No one's gonna be able to tell them apart but us—" Mig pointed to himself and his brother "—'cause we're twins."

"I need to check the mail in the bunkhouse," Mack said. "You guys behave for Beth."

Before it registered that she'd been left alone with the twins, the boys shoved more cookies into their mouths and waited for her to make the next move.

"What did you learn in school today?" she asked.

Miguel gulped his milk, then mumbled, "Nothing."

"I learned the three Rs," Javier said.

"That sounds stupid."

Javier glared at his brother.

"The three Rs." Beth tapped her finger against her chin. "I don't think I know what that means."

Javier took the bait. "Reuse, recycle and reduce."

Beth had expected Javier to say reading, writing and arithmetic.

"Mrs. Murphy said we have to take care of the earth and not litter and stuff."

"I don't get it," Miguel said.

"Mrs. Murphy said we're supposed to—"

The back door flew open. "Who wants to play catch?" Mack asked.

Bandit bolted outside and Miguel followed, leaving

his half-empty glass of milk behind. Javier remained at the table and continued eating.

"What else did Mrs. Murphy suggest we reuse?" Beth asked.

"She said we could refill our water bottles from the sink."

"That's smart. If everyone did that, we'd use fewer plastic bottles."

"And she said when we brush our teeth we should shut off the water until we're done spitting."

"Not wasting water is pretty important in the desert, isn't it?"

Javier nodded. "How come you know so much about stuff?"

"Like you, I listened to my teachers in school." When Javier remained silent, she asked, "Are you excited about your mom and dad bringing home your sisters?" The boy looked so forlorn that it was all Beth could do not to hug him.

"My dad says my mom's gonna be busy with the babies and we're not supposed to bother her."

"Babies are a lot of work."

"Do you have babies?"

Her breath caught in her throat. She'd been doing so well, answering Javier's questions while ignoring the fact that she found his company charming.

"What's the matter? You look sad."

She wanted to cry. "I'm fine." Her voice sounded rusty and she cleared her throat. "I don't have any children."

"Are you and Uncle Mack gonna have babies?"

The kitchen walls closed in on her and she struggled

to draw air into her lungs. "Your uncle and I are just friends, Javier."

"My dad and mom were friends and they got married."

"And look what a nice family you have," she said. "A mom, dad, brother and now two sisters."

"My cousin Ryan got a girlfriend. He never wants to play with me now."

"The whole boy-girl thing is complicated," she said. "You don't have to worry about girlfriends for a few years."

"Do you wanna see my reading book?" Javier reached into his backpack on the floor by the chair. "It's called—" he set the book on the table and pointed to each word on the cover "—Ben…and…Buster." Javier opened the book and read the first page.

Beth listened as she took in the room. There were signs of children everywhere—colored magnetic alphabet letters holding up pieces of artwork on the refrigerator door. Batman drinking cups sitting on the counter. A white ceramic cookie jar with small blue handprints and the words Happy Mother's Day painted on the side. Snack-size packages of treats filled a clear container on the counter and next to the back door sat two pairs of miniature cowboy boots.

"Let's go outside." Beth needed to get out of the house.

Javier glanced up, then quickly looked away but not before she saw his hurt expression. "I thought you could read on the swing," she said.

The sparkle returned to his eyes.

When she walked onto the porch, she breathed a sigh of relief—the trees, barn and Mack's truck didn't remind her of children. Mack's and Miguel's laughter met her ears, but they were nowhere in sight. Maybe they'd ventured into the pecan groves on the other side of the barn.

Javier tugged on her pant leg. "C'mon, let's sit down."

"Sure." When they sat on the swing, Javier pointed to her shoes.

"What?"

"Your feet don't touch."

She leaned forward. "Neither do yours."

Javier inched closer to Beth until his shoulder rubbed her arm. Would it really hurt to give the little guy a hug? She could do that without falling apart, couldn't she? She snuggled Javier against her side. "Go on. I'm listening."

Javier read, but Beth didn't hear a word. Her attention focused on the pecan groves until the trees became a blur of green and brown. She retreated inside herself to a dark corner that shielded her from the cold, hard world. The gloom closed in on her in a protective way, blocking the pain and emotional devastation that came with knowing she'd never have what most women had—children of their own. Yes, she'd contemplated adoption and yes, her own mother had even told her to stop feeling sorry for herself and adopt if she really wanted to experience motherhood, but Beth's fears had stopped her.

There were thousands of children waiting for a home…a couple to love them, but it wouldn't be the same as having her own child and gazing into the eyes of a son or daughter and seeing herself reflected back. And she worried that if she did adopt, the child would see through her and know that he or she was a substitute for what Beth really wanted.

She wasn't sure how long she and Javier had been sitting on the swing when Mack and Miguel entered the yard, Bandit trotting behind them. Miguel spoke and Mack's head fell back, his chest shaking with laughter. Then the dog jumped on Mack, knocking him to the ground. Miguel dove on top of his uncle and the two wrestled while Bandit danced in circles.

"I wanna play!" Javier dropped his book in Beth's lap and dashed off the porch. He raced across the lawn and joined in the fun.

Beth observed with a broken heart as the three rolled in the grassy dirt. A horn honked seconds before a pickup pulled up to the house and parked next to Mack's truck. A young woman got out of the passenger side and the man reached into the back and removed a child from a car seat.

"I thought you were going to the hospital." Mack walked over to the couple while the twins played with the dog.

"I hope you don't mind, but Nate has a cold and I didn't want to expose him to more germs at the hospital."

The woman must be Mack's sister. She pulled a tissue from her pocket and wiped the toddler's runny nose. "Can you handle watching him and the twins?"

"Sure. I have help." Mack waved Beth over.

If Beth had known a cattle-buying trip would evolve into running a daycare with Mack, she would have remained at the dude ranch.

"Beth, this is my sister, Dixie, and her husband,

Gavin." He pointed to the child. "And that little bucka-roo is Nate."

"Nice to meet you," Beth said.

"We won't stay at the hospital long." Dixie thrust her son at Beth, taking her by surprise. "I'm glad you're here. Mack's great with kids but Nate's a mama's boy and he'll want you."

Instinctively, Beth settled Nate on her hip. The toddler looked at her, his expression serious. She smiled at the tyke and a warm, cozy feeling filled her when the boy laid his head against her.

Gavin handed a diaper bag to Mack. "There's an extra set of clothes, his pajamas and food. Good luck."

"You better let us know when Isi has the babies," Mack said.

"We'll call." Dixie kissed Nate's forehead. "Be good, honey." Dixie looked at Beth. "Thank you for helping my brother with the kids."

Mack stood next to Beth, watching the truck's tail-lights disappear. If she allowed herself to, she could almost imagine she was holding her and Mack's son and they were a family.

"Uncle Mack! Can Nate play with us?" Miguel shouted.

"Nate doesn't feel good," Mack said.

"What should I do with him?" She didn't think it was a silly question but the grin on Mack's face told her he thought it was.

"Why don't you ask Nate what he wants to do?"

"Nate, how old are you?" she asked.

The boy held up three fingers. "What do you want to do?" He didn't answer. "Would you like to sit on the swing and watch the boys play?"

"Good choice," Mack said. "Nate likes the porch swing. He was a colicky baby and Gavin and Dix would sit outside and rock him for hours while he slept."

"I like swings, too," she said.

Mack jogged ahead of Beth and placed the diaper bag on the porch, then joined the soccer game in progress, leaving her alone with Nate.

Beth set him next to her on the swing, but he immediately crawled into her lap and rested his head against her chest. She ran her fingers through his fine, dark hair. Humming softly, she set the swing in motion. After a few minutes Nate fell asleep.

She wasn't sure how long she'd been holding him when the trio of soccer players appeared on the porch, dirty and tuckered out. Mack checked his watch. "It's six o'clock. Why don't the twins and I run into town and grab supper."

"What about Nate?" The child slept through their conversation.

Mack dug in the diaper bag and removed the plastic containers of food. "Dixie packed a bunch of healthy stuff for Nate. I'll get him chicken fingers. He likes those."

"That sounds good to me," she said.

The trio hopped into Mack's truck and drove off.

She continued to rock Nate, and her thoughts drifted back to adoption. Even though she'd been set against raising someone else's child, she'd found the courage to bring up the subject with Brad after they'd married. To her relief he'd wanted to concentrate on his career. She'd never shared her fears about adoption with her mother or Brad. Silly as it seemed, she worried that she wouldn't be able to form a bond with a child that wasn't a part of her. She'd heard stories of couples who'd adopted and had devoted their lives to making the child happy, then years later the child blamed them for the poor decisions they'd made or the unfortunate circumstances they were in. Beth understood that the same thing could happen to parents with their biological children, but she believed the risks weren't as high.

She snuggled Nate closer, the long day catching up with her. She closed her eyes, intending to rest for a few minutes. A horn blast startled her and her eyes popped open. She felt disoriented until she remembered she was at the farm helping Mack with his nephews. Nate slept through the noise of Mack's truck pulling into the yard and the twins piling out, talking a mile a minute.

When they reached the porch, Mack handed the fast-food bags to Miguel. "Take this inside and both of you wash your hands." He walked over to the swing. "Conway called and asked if I'd spend the night with the boys so he can stay at the hospital with Isi. After Dixie picks up Nate I can drive you out to the dude ranch."

She didn't want Mack to have to make the long drive that late at night with the twins. "I don't mind staying. I can sleep on the couch."

"Great."

Nothing was going to happen between her and Mack with the twins around.

He nodded to Nate. "I'll watch him. You go eat."

"Are you sure?"

Mack lifted his nephew into his arms and took Beth's seat when she vacated the swing. "I'm a pro at this."

To Beth's way of thinking, Mack was a pro at a lot of things.

Chapter Ten

"Uncle Mack, are you gonna marry Beth?" Javier asked after the boys climbed into the bathtub.

"Javi wants to know 'cause he's gonna marry Stephanie," Mig said.

"Am not."

Amused by the red splotches spreading across Javi's cheeks, Mack asked, "Who's Stephanie?"

"His girlfriend." Mig giggled. "They swing together at recess."

"We do not." Javi pretended interest in a mound of soap bubbles.

"Is Stephanie nice?"

"Yeah," Javi said. "She's really smart. The teacher picks her first when she raises her hand."

Mack wondered if Isi and Conway knew their shy son was sweet on a girl. He'd bet they didn't.

"So are you gonna marry Beth, Uncle Mack?" Javier asked again.

Mack cupped his hands and sent a big splash at their heads. The boys ducked and the bath water hit the tiled wall. Miguel joined in the fun and slapped the surface of the water, soaking the front of Mack's shirt.

"Uh-oh!" Javi pulled his brother to his side of the tub.

A water war ensued, all three becoming drenched. "Stop!" Mack held his hands up in surrender. "Your dad's going to be mad if the water on the floor leaks into the kitchen."

A snuffle sounded outside the door. "Let Bandit in," Miguel said.

Mack glanced at the puddles on the floor. He supposed the four-legged mutt couldn't make much more of a mess than the boys had. He opened the door and in less than a second Bandit assessed the situation then bounded past Mack and jumped into the water. Miguel grabbed the edge of the tub and spared himself a dunking, but the dog knocked Javi under the water. Mack pulled the kid up for air and he sputtered and coughed. "You okay, buddy?"

"Bad dog, Bandit." Javi hugged the Lab's neck.

"That scolding will teach him not to jump into the tub." Mack handed Mig the bottle of dog shampoo from beneath the sink. "Might as well wash him while he's in there." The boys poured half the bottle on the Lab. Bandit flung his head back and forth, sending globs of lather flying across the room. It would take an hour to clean up after all three dried off.

"Did you wash your hair?" Mack asked Mig. The kid shook his head. "You do your own or does your mother help?"

"She helps 'cause we don't scrub hard enough," Javi said.

"Wash each other's hair." Mack leaned against the closed door and watched the boys squirt dog shampoo on their heads, then create Mohawk hairstyles. "That's not scrubbing."

The boys ignored him, so he got out his iPhone. "Look this way." He snapped a photo of the trio then sent it to Conway. "Your dad will get a kick out of you three mutts."

"We're not mutts," Mig said.

"That's up for debate. Pull the plug and don't move." He opened the door and stuck his head into the hall. "Beth?"

The boards on the stairs popped and creaked, then a moment later she appeared on the landing. "Will you fetch a pitcher or a bowl I can use to rinse the boys off with?"

"Sure." Beth rummaged through the kitchen cupboards until she found a plastic juice pitcher. When she delivered the container to Mack, she gaped at the scene in the bathroom.

"Look, Uncle Mack." Javi pointed to the doorway. "Aunt Beth's catching flies."

"That's what Uncle Porter says to Javi 'cause he never shuts his mouth," Mig said.

"He says that to you, too." Javi pushed his brother.

"No shoving in the tub." Mack took the pitcher. "Thanks."

While the boys argued, the words *Aunt Beth* wrapped her in a warm hug and a yearning sensation grabbed hold of her heart, squeezing until her chest ached.

This was what it would be like to have children—the amusement, the messes and the love. It was missing out on the love that bothered her most about never having a child of her own.

"Shoot," Mack said. "I forgot to call Dave and tell him we wouldn't be back tonight."

"I spoke to him," Beth said. "He wants you to let him know in the morning if you need to stay here and help with the boys."

"Aunt Beth." Miguel shivered in his towel.

"Yes, Mig?"

"Can we camp outside in a tent?"

"Wait a minute, guys—"

"Sure. As long as you go to sleep when Uncle Mack says. You can't miss the school bus in the morning." Beth smiled at Mack's incredulous stare. "I'd better check on Nate." The toddler had been sleeping for the past hour in the family room.

"Uncle Mack." Mig's voice floated into the hallway and she paused on the landing. "I like Aunt Beth. She's cool."

"Yeah, she's way cool," Javi said.

"I agree." Mack's deeper voice sent shivers down her spine. "Aunt Beth is *way* cool."

Back in the family room Beth read a magazine article on homemade remedies for laundry stains. Fifteen minutes later the boys and Mack came downstairs, grabbed a snack then went outside to pitch a tent in the yard. Nate made soft snoring sounds from his bed on the couch and soon Beth drifted off to sleep with him.

"Shh…"

The whispered hush woke Beth and she sat up quickly, the magazine in her lap falling to the floor.

"I'm sorry." Dixie offered a smile as she approached the couch and peered at her son. "I didn't mean to startle you."

"Nate fell asleep after supper," Beth said. "He didn't eat much, but he did drink a glass of milk."

"That's fine." Dixie felt his head. "He's warm again."

"Is that bad?"

"He's been running a low-grade fever for the past two days. I think we're going to take the doctor's advice and have tubes put in his ears."

"I've heard of children having trouble with ear infections," Beth said.

Dixie lifted her sleeping son into her arms and snuggled him close. "This little cowboy has given me fits since day one. Colicky and never-ending ear infections, but if he grows up to be just like his daddy, then I'm not complaining." Dixie's love for her husband echoed strongly in her voice.

"Did Mack tell you about the girls?" Dixie asked.

"No."

"They each weighed a little over five pounds. They're tiny like their mother and they both have her dark hair."

"Have they decided on names?"

"Emma and Molly."

"Pretty names," Beth said.

She picked up the magazine and set it on the coffee table. "I should see if Mack needs help with the boys."

Dixie trailed Beth through the house. "Conway said to tell you and Mack that he'd make it back to the farm tomorrow before the bus brought the boys home from school."

"I made the twins lunches, and I checked their backpacks for any notes from their teachers." Beth walked onto the back porch.

"Mack would never have thought to look in their

backpacks. Sounds like you have everything under control." Dixie descended the steps.

"Wait. You forgot the diaper bag." Beth fetched the tote from the kitchen and handed it to Dixie. Then she got her first good look at the tent. The shelter listed slightly to the right, one side of the canvas sagging. Flashlights inside the tent illuminated the boys' shadows as they moved about.

Mack and his brother-in-law stood next to the pickups looking at pictures on their phones.

"Beth, did you see the girls?" Mack asked when she and Dixie joined them. He ran his finger across the bottom of the phone, revealing several photos of the happy couple and the newborns.

"They're sweethearts," Beth said.

"Check out the photo I sent Conway." Mack showed his phone to his sister.

"Mack!" Dixie snorted. "Thank God Beth was here to help with Nate. No way am I ever leaving *you* alone with my son."

"Hey, I'm a great babysitter." Mack glanced at Beth for confirmation. "Right?"

"I don't know about great," she said. "But the boys love you."

Gavin took Nate from Dixie and put him in his child seat, then the couple got into their truck and drove off.

"Beth."

"What?"

Mack clasped her face between his hands, his breath puffing against her lips. "Thank you for helping me with the boys. I couldn't have asked for a better sidekick than you." He kissed her—not the slow, gentle caress she'd been dreaming about for hours but a hot, deep, lusty, I-want-you kiss.

There was no mistaking the hardening bulge nudging her stomach, and she wished they could send the twins inside to their beds and commandeer the tent for themselves. When they came up for air, he said, "The more I kiss you, the more I want to."

Beth felt the same.

"Come join us in the tent. There's plenty of room."

"One of us needs a decent night's sleep in order to get the twins ready for school in the morning."

"Are you always this sensible?"

"Of course." She nodded. "I'll say good-night to the boys." She walked away from Mack—while she still could—and rapped her knuckles on the canvas. "Knock, knock."

The zipper lowered and two heads poked out.

"I wanted to say good-night."

"You're not gonna sleep with us?" Javi asked.

"I'm afraid not." She bent over and whispered, "But you two are going to have to take care of your uncle because he's afraid of the dark."

Miguel's gaze shifted to Mack, who was texting on his phone. "He is?"

"Yep. But don't tell him I told you." She kept a straight face at their befuddled expressions. "As long as you sleep real close to him and hold his hand he'll be fine."

"Okay," Javi said. "We won't let him be afraid." The boys retreated inside the tent then Beth spoke to Mack. "Where should I sleep tonight?"

He shoved the phone into his pocket. "You can take

one of the boys' beds. Isi keeps clean sheets in the linen closet at the end of the hallway."

"I hate to mess up their bed for one night. The couch is fine."

"Isi wouldn't want you to sleep on the couch after helping me take care of her sons."

"Fine. I'll pick a bed."

He leaned in and kissed her. "Dream about me."

After that kiss she didn't have any choice.

"How'd I get tricked into helping you again?" Porter maneuvered the wire stretcher into place and pulled the barbed wire taut, then Mack stapled it to the post.

"You don't have a job. That's why you're here." Mack whipped off his hat and rubbed his shirtsleeve across his brow. The fifty head of cattle from the Still Water Ranch were scheduled to arrive in a couple of days and he and Porter were installing the final leg of fencing to prevent the herd from wandering off to Mexico when Mack's back was turned.

"I interviewed for a job last week," Porter said.

"Oh, yeah?" Mack admired their handiwork, his eyes searching for a weak spot in the twelve-foot span. "Where?"

"Del Mar Rodeo Productions."

"What would you do for them?"

"Haul bulls to rodeos."

"Seriously? You're going to give up rodeo to drive a cattle rig?" Porter was a decent rodeo cowboy. If he put his mind to it, he'd make good money on the circuit, but he got sidetracked by all the pretty women and couldn't concentrate worth a damn.

"Hey, you guys are always telling me I need to think about the future and find steady employment."

"Yeah, but a job delivering bulls?"

"The owner says I can compete in the rodeos I deliver the bulls to as long as I don't deviate from the schedule."

"When do you start?" Mack asked.

"I haven't gotten the job yet." Porter grinned. "If they hire me as a driver it'll be a temporary position."

Mack busted up laughing.

"What's so funny?"

"How temporary?" One week was Porter's usual M.O.

"A few months. I'll show you that I can stick to a job."

Mack read the seriousness in his brother's eyes. "Okay, I'll bite. Why this job? Why now?"

Porter shuffled his feet. "Maybe because my siblings are all tying the knot and settling down."

"I'm still single."

"Not for long." Porter handed the wire stretcher to Mack. "Hoss said you and Beth stayed overnight in Prescott. Are things becoming serious between you two?"

"Maybe." It sure felt like it on his part, but Mack wasn't as certain Beth's feelings for him were traveling down the same road.

"What's her story? Hoss said you two had met before she showed up at the ranch." Porter snapped his fingers and his eyes widened. "No way. She's the Just Beth you talked about that afternoon in the bunkhouse."

Mack wouldn't mind sharing with Porter, but Beth

was a private person, and she wouldn't want his brother knowing the details of their one-night stand.

"Beth used to be married to the sportscaster for Channel 3."

"Brad Stevens?"

"That's the—" *jerk* "—guy."

"Why'd they divorce?"

"Same reasons most people get divorced."

"Which one cheated?" Porter asked.

"Stevens cheated with Beth's boss."

"Ouch." Porter frowned. "That means you're her rebound guy."

Acid churned in Mack's stomach. As much as he wanted to believe he wasn't Beth's boy toy, she'd given him no reason to suggest otherwise. As a matter of fact she'd tried to tell him that he wasn't her forever guy the morning after in Prescott.

"Did I hit a nerve?" Porter asked. "I'm sorry, I didn't—"

Mack walked to the pickup and hopped in, then drove it to where they'd set the last fence post. He hauled another post from the truck bed and dropped it on the ground. When Porter caught up, he said, "I'm thinking we should reinforce this section."

The fence didn't require an additional post but the frustration that had been building inside Mack needed an outlet. He and Beth hadn't had any privacy since they'd returned from Prescott. First they had to take care of the twins, and then the next group of guests arrived at the dude ranch, and he had to entertain three families while Beth remained hidden away in her cabin. And as soon as the guests departed this morning, he and Porter had gone out to finish the fence.

Mack was suffering from severe Beth withdrawal.

His brother's phone went off but Mack barely heard the conversation. After Porter hung up, he said, "That was Conway. He wants to know when we're coming to see the girls."

Tonight would be the only time Mack could squeeze in a visit to the farm. "I'll head out there later." He'd ask Beth to go with him.

"We've got company." Porter pointed into the distance.

As Hoss's truck drew closer, Mack spotted Beth behind the wheel. His heart stumbled, then regained its balance and beat hard inside his chest. "Take a hike, Porter."

"We're in the middle of the desert."

Mack grinned. "Go look for water."

Porter picked up the post digger and went off to dig.

When Beth stopped the truck, Mack approached the driver's-side window. "Mornin'." She looked so damned good—probably because he hadn't been this close to her in days.

"What's Porter doing?" she asked.

"Staying out of earshot."

"Why?"

"So I can do this." Mack stuck his head through the window and planted an intimate kiss on her lips.

When he pulled away, she fumbled with the picnic basket on the seat next to her. "I brought lunch."

"Thanks." He loved that his kisses made her blush. "How would you like to go with me tonight to see Conway and Isi's girls?"

"I'm afraid I'm busy."

There had been no hesitation in her answer and

Mack was surprised she didn't want to see the newborns. "What are you doing?"

"Filling out a job application," she said.

"Where?"

"In my cabin."

"No, where's the job located?" he asked.

"San José."

"California?"

"Yes, California. I have to find a job. I can't live at the dude ranch forever."

February first was two days away—the month had flown by. "You can spare a few hours to visit a pair of cute babies, can't you?"

"I'm sorry, but I—"

"Mig and Javi miss you." He knew Beth had a soft spot for the boys, especially Javi, who had latched on to her when they'd spent the night at the farm with them. "Don't you want to hear what they think of their new sisters?"

She cracked a smile, then it quickly faded. "I'm sure the boys love the babies."

"Come with me."

"I can't."

Can't? "Sure you can." He motioned to the fence. "As soon as Porter and I string the rest of the wire, we'll leave."

"I really don't think—"

Mack leaned inside the window for a second kiss, but Beth stiffened. "What's wrong?"

She wouldn't make eye contact with him and he got a sick feeling in his gut—she was pulling away.

He tugged off his leather gloves, then grasped her chin and turned her head toward him, forcing her to meet his gaze. "Isi wants to thank you for helping me with the boys. Please come with me."

His stomach twisted tighter as he watched the struggle in her eyes. She really didn't want to go with him. He tried to back off, but fear that he was losing her wouldn't let him. "I'll knock on your cabin door when I'm ready." He didn't want to give her a chance to say no again, so he grabbed the picnic basket and said, "Thanks for bringing us lunch." When he moved away from the truck, she took off like a bat out of hell. Mack walked over to Porter. "Beth brought us lunch."

"Yeah, it looked like she wanted to give you more than food."

"Jealous?" Mack grinned even though deep down he suspected Beth was serious about putting distance between them.

Porter opened his mouth but nothing came out. Then he scowled and muttered, "Shut up." He fished a sandwich from the basket and took a huge bite.

"We're finishing this fence pronto," Mack said.

"Eager to see the babies?" Porter asked.

"Sure." That was partly the truth. But Mack also felt a desperate need to keep Beth within arm's reach. Yes, she'd been honest with him from the get-go, claiming that she'd consider all her options when she searched for a new job. But it hurt that after the time they'd spent together she still wasn't ruling out moving away from Yuma. And him.

Chapter Eleven

"They're beautiful girls, Isi." The infants slept side by side in one of the cribs. The nursery walls had been painted pink and sported a paper border of dancing ballerinas. A pink rug covered the wood floor, and both cribs, a rocking chair, dresser and changing table had been painted a glossy white. The room shone with love.

"They're precious," Isi said, "but I know from experience that they're a lot of work the first few years." She motioned for Beth to follow her, and the women returned to the kitchen, where Isi made tea. "I can't believe I'm done having children and you haven't even begun."

The innocent comment sliced through Beth, and she dropped her gaze to the dark liquid in her mug.

"I guess that's what happens when you have two babies at once," Isi said.

"It's nice that Miguel and Javier will help look after the girls as they grow up."

Isi set a plate of cookies on the table. "Help yourself. I have four canisters of homemade treats in the freezer." She raised her hands in surrender. "Why is it that everyone brings you sweets when you have kids, and that's the last thing the boys should be eating so much of?"

Beth's face heated and Isi laughed. "Your box of candy doesn't count. That's for me. I don't share chocolate."

Beth had wanted to bring Isi a welcome-home-from-the-hospital gift but the only place to buy anything on the way to the farm had been the gas station convenience store in Stagecoach where she'd purchased the box of Valentine's Day candy.

"Are you always this quiet?" Isi asked.

Beth couldn't very well tell Mack's sister-in-law that she was jealous of her or that she'd give anything to trade places with her. "It's been a long day, and I'm tired."

"Wait until you have your first baby. Then you'll really know what tired feels like."

A squawk from the baby monitor on the counter interrupted them. Isi bolted from her chair. "They're hungry again." She offered an apologetic smile and left the kitchen.

The back door opened and Miguel appeared. "Where's my mom?"

"Upstairs taking care of your sisters."

He eyed the cookies on the table.

"Would you like one, Miguel?" Beth pushed the plate toward him.

He reached for a cookie but stopped and looked at Beth. "I gotta wash my hands, don't I?"

"That's probably a good idea."

He went into the hall bathroom. While he washed up, Beth poured him a glass of milk.

"Thank you," he said when he returned to the kitchen and sat down. He shoved half a cookie into his mouth then mumbled, "You can call me Mig." His eyes strayed to the monitor when one of the babies whimpered.

"What do you think of your new sisters?"

"They stink."

Beth laughed. "I thought babies smelled sweet and were soft and cuddly."

"They smell like poop." Miguel shoved the rest of the cookie in his mouth and swallowed. "You should see my dad's face when he changes their diapers."

"What does Bandit think of the babies?"

"He sniffs them a lot, but he'd rather play outside with me and Javi."

The dog was one hundred percent loyal to the boys. Beth suspected that as the girls grew older, Bandit would pick playing soccer over tea parties.

"What's Javi up to?" Beth hadn't seen him since she and Mack had arrived at the farm.

"He's in the bunkhouse playing poker with Uncle Porter and my dad." Miguel grabbed a second cookie. "Uncle Porter says Uncle Mack's never here to play anymore. He's always at the dude ranch."

"Oh?" Was Mack choosing to stay at the dude ranch because she never left? Beth worried he was reading too much into their relationship.

And whose fault is that?

"Aunt Beth?"

"Call me Beth, honey." She didn't want the boys to get the impression that she and Mack were a couple— at least not long-term.

"Do you like my uncle Mack?"

"Of course I do." What was there not to like about the cowboy? He was handsome, fun, sexy, hard-working and he loved his family. In her eyes, Mack was darn near perfect.

"Uncle Porter says Uncle Mack's got the hots for you. What does that mean?"

Ugh. This is exactly why she hadn't wanted to go with Mack to the farm. Getting too close to his family would make it all the more difficult to move on—to wherever the future took her. "Your Uncle Porter should keep his comments to himself."

"Huh?"

"Never mind."

"I know!" Miguel sat up straight in the chair. "It means Uncle Mack's gonna marry you, right?"

An ache spread through Beth, and she had to swallow twice before she found her voice. "No, honey. Your uncle and I are not getting married. We're just friends."

"Hey, Mig." Mack's voice drifted through the screen door. Had he been eavesdropping on the porch?

The door opened and Mack's sober expression answered her question. "Go check on your brother."

"Javi's playing cards with—"

"Then go play cards." Mack scowled. "Now, Mig."

The boy grabbed two cookies. "They're for Javi," he said, scooting out the door.

"Let's take a walk."

Beth had known she couldn't avoid this conversation forever and she was ashamed that she hadn't been better at resisting the urge to be with Mack. But she'd convinced herself that they were both just having fun and had blocked out the voice in her head that claimed there could never be a long-term commitment between them. Mack held the door open and she stepped onto the porch. He clasped her hand. Funny how his warm grip gave her the courage to do the right thing—break his heart.

As he led her across the yard, she asked, "What happened to Bandit's doghouse?" There was a chunk of wood missing from the overhang and it listed slightly to the right.

"A bad storm blew through here last summer. The winds picked up the doghouse and slammed it into Conway's truck." Mack didn't offer any details about the incident.

Beth peeked sideways at him when they entered the orchard. The nerve along his jaw pulsed angrily, and a queasy feeling gripped her stomach. This was all her fault. Her first mistake had been waiting for Mack outside the Number 10 Saloon, which led her to going to the El Rancho Motel with him. Her second mistake had been staying at the dude ranch after she discovered Mack worked there. And her third mistake had been accompanying him on the drive to Prescott and spending the night in a hotel with him.

So many mistakes...

He veered left onto a narrow path at the edge of the grove. "Where are we going?"

"To the graveyard."

Graveyard? Fifty yards in the distance she spotted an iron gate. As they approached the enclosure shaded by a large pecan tree, she counted four markers. "Who's buried here?"

"My grandparents, mother and Dixie's daughter."

Beth gasped. "I didn't know your sister had had another child."

"She miscarried a baby girl and named her after our grandmother." Mack entered the family plot, walked over to his mother's grave and pulled a weed next to the headstone. He motioned to the far corner of the enclosure. "Lucky's buried there."

"A family pet?"

"Grandpa wouldn't let us have a dog when we were kids and we never understood why until Grandma Ada told us that when Grandpa had been a teenager he accidentally ran over their family dog, Buster. Grandma said he was so heartbroken he never wanted another one."

"How did Lucky end up here?"

"My brothers and I were hiking in the desert when we spotted the dog. He was skin and bones. We snuck food out of the house for him and made sure he had water, but he kept his distance from the farm."

"Did you ever get him to go home with you?"

"No. I think Lucky knew our grandfather wouldn't welcome him."

"And your grandmother never found out you were feeding a stray?"

"She knew, but she felt bad that Grandpa wouldn't let us have a pet so she turned a blind eye to what we were doing."

"Were you ever able to get close to Lucky?"

"Not until he was dying. Johnny found him lying behind the barn, barely alive. That was the first time he'd ever come near the property."

"That's sad, but he was fortunate that you made his last days better."

"We took turns sitting with him until the end. Then we carried him out here and buried him." Mack smiled. "I remember Grandpa coming into the house for supper one day and mentioning a suspicious-looking mound in the graveyard. When he asked us kids if we knew anything about it, Grandma said she'd planted wildflower seeds to brighten our mother's grave. We figured then that Grandma knew we'd buried the dog."

"What did your grandfather say when the wildflowers didn't appear?"

"Funny thing," Mack said. "That spring the graveyard was overrun with flowers." His expression grew serious. "I didn't bring you out here to talk about Lucky."

The short reprieve had ended—now she had to face the music.

"Why did you tell Mig that you and I are just friends? You know there's a lot more going on between us than friendship."

"Mack, I'm sorry if I led you to believe our relationship was more than…than—"

"What, Beth? A fling? A temporary affair?"

The oxygen seeped from her lungs, leaving her head spinning.

Say it.

If she loved Mack she had to let him go—for his sake. The past few weeks, a tiny part of her heart had begun to believe he might learn to love her enough that he'd be willing to give up fatherhood. Then they'd taken care of the twins the night Isi gave birth and he'd shown her how much he enjoyed his nephews. The way he'd joked with the boys while they took their bath had touched Beth deeply. And Mack never lost his patience with the twins—it was as if his nephews had been as much his sons as his brother's. It had saddened and hurt Beth to watch him interact with the boys because it reminded her that even if they stayed together, she'd never be able to watch Mack be a father to a child she gave birth to. If there was ever a man meant to have his own children it was Mack. Beth wanted him to have that family, even if it was with someone else. "I'm sorry."

"Sorry for what?"

"I thought you understood." *Oh, God, why was this so hard?* "We've had a lot of fun together but—"

"I was your rebound guy? You used me to scratch a sexual itch?"

He didn't have to make what they'd shared sound crude. Eyes burning she fought tears and forced the lie from her mouth. "Yes."

His eyes sparked with anger then he looked away, clenching and unclenching his hands at his sides.

She hated that she'd hurt him. "I like you, Mack. You're—"

"Like?" He glared at her. "I feel a lot more than like for you, Beth."

His words hardened her heart—she had to do this. "I'm leaving Yuma at the end of February." And in case he was wondering… "Whether I get the job in San José or not." She couldn't remain in the area. Her heart would break to pieces if she ran into him and another woman—or worse—him and his child.

"Seriously?" Mack spread his arms wide. "What we shared was nothing more than a fun time?"

She hated that she'd hurt him, but if she told the truth—that she'd fallen in love with him—he'd squeeze past her defenses and claim more of her heart than he'd already stolen. And it would take little effort on his part to convince her to give them a chance. Then when she told him she couldn't have children, he'd feel sorry for her, and the last thing she wanted was a man staying with her out of pity. No matter how deep Mack's love for her, eventually he'd change his mind about wanting children, and she was determined to spare them both that kind of pain.

"Mack—"

"Is it because I'm in the band? Are you afraid I'll stray?" She opened her mouth to deny the charge, but he spoke over her. "I'm done with the band."

"You can't quit playing your music. You're too talented."

"I don't need a band to play my music. Besides, all of us are moving on with our lives." He closed the distance between them and brushed a strand of hair out of her eyes, his fingers lingering against her cheek.

She savored his closeness, knowing there would be no more gentle caresses from him.

"The ink on your divorce papers wasn't even dry when we met, but I know what I feel for you. I'll wait as long as I need to until you're ready to take the next step with me."

His declaration broke her heart in half. Why was he making this so difficult? "There isn't going to be a next step, Mack."

He released her. "I don't understand."

"You're not listening to me." If she wasn't brutal, he would see through her. "I never wanted anything more from you than a temporary affair."

Mack picked up a rock from the ground and threw it at the trunk of the pecan tree. "I thought you were different. You may not dress like a buckle bunny but you're as self-centered as one."

She deserved the insult and a whole lot more. "It'll be dark soon," she said. "We'd better return to the dude ranch." She couldn't look him in the eye, so she edged past him and walked along the trail by herself.

When Mack entered the yard a few minutes later, he said his goodbyes and acted as if nothing was wrong. They made the ride to the ranch in silence, except when Mack asked if she was hungry. She declined the offer to stop and grab a bite to eat, and when he finally parked in front of the ranch office, she couldn't escape the confines of the pickup fast enough. Once she entered her cabin, she locked the door—in case Mack decided to plead his case once more.

She fixed herself a cup of tea then flipped on the TV. She'd survive this. She'd survived losing her marriage. Losing her job.

Losing Mack was another one of life's disappointments she'd survive, too.

Then the tears came—not a few, but a river of grief poured from her eyes.

"YER AS FULL of venom as a rattlesnake in August," Hoss said.

Mack ignored the coot and stabbed the pitchfork into the soiled hay, then flung the clump of manure into the wheelbarrow outside Speckles's stall.

"You gonna keep pretendin' I ain't here?"

"Leave me alone, Hoss. I'm pissed as hell, and I don't want to be messed with." Two days had passed since Beth had ended their relationship, and he'd yet to make sense of it.

"I'm guessin' yer meanness has somethin' to do with Beth leavin'."

Mack's lungs froze in the middle of drawing a breath. "She left?"

"She put her luggage in her car and drove off 'bout two hours ago."

Beth had left without saying goodbye. He might have only been her *fling* but he deserved a goodbye. "I'll finish mucking the stalls later." Mack left the barn and headed to Dave's office. He didn't bother to knock. "Hoss said Beth left."

Dave glanced up from the ledger in front of him. "She took off this morning."

"Did she say where she was going?"

"She's got a job interview in San José, and then she'd planned to visit her parents for a day or two." Dave's eyes narrowed. "Why?"

He forced himself to ask the next question. "Is she coming back?"

"She didn't say, but I told her she could stay here as long as she wants."

Panic swept through Mack because the past forty-eight hours he'd been plagued by memories of Beth, and he swore she cared more about him than she professed to.

Maybe you just can't let go.

A horn blast drew him to the office window, where he spotted a livestock trailer pulling up to the corral. "The cattle are here." Forcing Beth to the back of his mind he and Dave headed outside.

"We're going to split the herd into two groups and put them in separate corrals, then Hoss and I can check them over for injuries before we let them loose to graze," Mack said.

While Dave spoke with the driver, Mack entered the barn. "Hoss, the cattle are here."

"I heard the truck." The old man pulled on his leather gloves and frowned.

"What?"

"Are you in the right frame of mind for workin' cattle, or do I have to worry 'bout you doin' somethin' stupid and gettin' yer head stomped?"

Mack opened his mouth to spew a lie then changed his mind. He didn't know if venting would help but it might settle his nerves before he went into a pen full of restless livestock. "Apparently, Beth didn't view our relationship the way I did."

"She dumped you, huh?"

Leave it to Hoss to get right to the point. "She said she was only looking for a fling."

"What were you lookin' for?"

"At first the same thing, but then…" After they'd made love, he'd felt a deeper connection to Beth and knew there was more between them than sex.

Hoss cleared his throat. "She don't seem like a gal who sleeps with every Tom, Dick and Harry."

Mack hadn't thought so, either. "She recently divorced and the night I met her she was celebrating her single status. We ended up at a motel, but she left before I woke the next morning."

"I'm sure she wasn't the first one-night stand you had." Hoss pulled a bandanna from his back pocket and tied it around his neck.

"I haven't had as many one-nighters as you might think. There was something different about Beth that night. She didn't act like a typical buckle bunny."

"Must have been plenty surprised to run into her at the ranch."

That was for sure.

"Is she comin' back?"

"I don't know. She's at a job interview in California."

"Seems like you still have a chance."

"To do what?"

"Prove to her that yer more 'n a pretty face."

The way Beth had made it sound, all that mattered was his pretty face. An image of her snuggled against his side flashed through his brain. He closed his eyes, and her voice echoed in his ears… *You make me feel safe, Mack.*

If he made her feel safe, why was she running from him?

"Let's go." Hoss hobbled out of the barn on his bowed legs.

Once the cattle truck was in position, Mack opened the trailer doors and lowered the ramp. When all fifty head were counted, he entered the corral and smacked his hat against his thigh, encouraging half the group to exit into the adjoining pen. "What do you think?" he asked Dave.

"They look healthy." The boss nodded to the renegade steer butting his head against rails. "You'll have to watch that one with the guests."

"We'll make sure he behaves or he won't go along on the drives. You heard anything from Jake? I'll need his help moving the cattle into the pasture."

"He hasn't called. Could be a week or two months before we see him again."

Great. "Any word from Millie?"

"Nope." Dave scuffed his boot against the ground.

"I'm sorry." Mack sure as hell knew what Dave was feeling. They should change the name of the place to

Heartbreak Ranch—anyone who stays here leaves with a broken heart.

"If Jake doesn't show up before we do our first cattle drive, tell Porter he's got the job, if he wants it." Dave gestured to Mack. "Are you and the band playing this weekend?"

"No. The guys want to be with their families, so we're cutting back on our performances." And Mack needed to focus on making the cattle drive a successful part of the dude ranch experience. He didn't have time to wallow in self-pity. Besides, it was Beth's loss if she couldn't see how perfect they were together.

Chapter Twelve

"Well, this is a surprise." Beth's mother opened the screen door and hugged her. "Why didn't you call ahead and tell us you were coming for a visit?" She ushered Beth into the house.

"I was in the neighborhood and I didn't want to leave California without seeing you." It was time to break the news about her divorce and she hoped her mother felt well enough to hear it.

"Come into the kitchen. I'll make lunch. Your father's golfing, but he'll be home soon."

"How are you feeling?" Beth asked.

"Much better. I've got my energy back from all those nasty radiation treatments." Her mother nodded to the pantry. "There's a bottle of merlot on the shelf." She opened the fridge and removed a plastic container. "I made chicken salad the other day."

"I'm glad you're feeling more like your old self now." Beth poured two glasses of wine and drank from one. "This is excellent."

Her mother raised an eyebrow. "The least you could do is sip and not guzzle."

"It's been a long…nine months, Mom."

"Oh, dear. Hold your thoughts until lunch is ready,

then I'm all ears." When her mother delivered the sand-wiches to the table, Beth had already finished a second serving of wine.

There was no way to ease into the subject, so she blurted, "Brad and I are officially divorced."

Her mother choked on her wine.

"Sorry. I should have waited until you swallowed." Beth patted her back. "I meant to tell you and Dad ear-lier but I didn't want to add to your worries when you were in the middle of your treatments."

"Honey, you should have told me anyway."

"Brad caught me off guard and it's taken a while to come to grips with everything."

"I can't say that I'm surprised." Her mother offered a sympathetic smile.

"Really?"

"When we first met Brad, I didn't have a good feel-ing about him. He was too cocky. Too self-centered, but your father warned me not share my impressions with you."

"I know Dad was excited that I was marrying a sportscaster." She recalled the evening they'd met her parents at a restaurant in San Diego and announced their engagement. Afterward, the dinner conversation had focused on sports until the check arrived, then Beth and her mother returned home, and her father and Brad had gone to a bar to talk more sports.

"Never mind your father. What happened?"

Beth didn't care to go into detail about how she and Brad had steadily grown apart the past five years, so she settled on the facts. "He slept with my boss."

Her mother winced.

"Brad met Sara at our company party."

"How long were they carrying on before you found out?"

This part of the story made Beth look like an idiot. "Several months. Then Sara became pregnant and Brad asked me for a divorce."

"I thought Brad didn't want children."

"He didn't, until Sara got pregnant. Then he decided fatherhood was a great idea. Evidently, the station manager believed Brad's ratings would go up if viewers perceived him as a family man."

"What a schmuck."

Beth appreciated her mother taking her side and squeezed her hand.

"You two could have adopted."

Her eyes burned, and Beth cursed herself for being weak. She'd cried enough tears over her failed marriage. "I feel sorry for Sara. She'll learn soon enough that the man she married is a self-centered, egotistical bastard."

And Mack is none of those things. Even now, sitting in her mother's kitchen after a stressful job interview and talking about her divorce, Mack was never far from her thoughts. If only the memory she carried in her heart wasn't the one of him gaping at her in stunned silence when she'd told him he'd been nothing more to her than a good time.

"Have they married?"

Her mother's voice interrupted Beth's daydream. "What?"

"I asked if Brad married your boss."

"Yes."

"How have you been holding up at work?"

"I quit my job. That's why I'm in California. I had an interview in San José yesterday."

"I wish you would have told me sooner. You're welcome to stay here with us as long as you need to."

"I knew you'd want me to come home if I'd told you. I didn't want to add more stress to your lives than you were already under."

"Well, I'm feeling fine now, so why don't you move in with us until you decide what to do?"

"I will if I need to, Mom."

"What about your place in Yuma?"

"We sold the house."

"Then where are you living?"

"Dad's friend, Dave Paxton, is letting me stay at—"

"The Black Jack Mountain Dude Ranch? Good grief, there's no need to stay at that desert hideaway."

"I thought you liked the dude ranch. You and dad go there once a year."

"Your father enjoys pretending he's a cowboy every now and then. He rides the trails and I sit in the cabin and catch up on my reading."

"I needed time alone to come to grips with the divorce and make plans for the future. The peace and quiet at the ranch has helped me." Excluding falling in love with Mack.

"You're a sensible girl. You'll land on your feet and be stronger for having gone through this."

Her mother wouldn't consider her daughter *sensible* if she knew Beth had had a one-night stand with Mack—a two-night stand if she counted the stay in Prescott. "To tell you the truth, I've enjoyed a break from the finance world." She squirmed under her mother's stare. "What?"

"You met a cowboy, didn't you?"

Drat. She hadn't intended on mentioning Mack.

"Where's your cowboy from?"

Mack wasn't her cowboy, but since her mother refused to drop the subject, she might as well confess everything—except the parts where she slept with Mack. After droning on for ten minutes, she allowed her mother a chance to speak.

"I'm surprised that you fell for another man who craves the limelight."

"I haven't fallen for Mack, Mom. We're just friends."

"Mack? Is he the cowboy who works for Dave?"

Beth nodded. She should have expected that her parents would recognize his name if they'd vacationed at the ranch.

"What's his last name? I don't recall it."

"His birth name is Merle Haggard Cash."

Her mother's mouth dropped open.

"He and his brothers were all named after country-and-western legends by their mother, who is now deceased."

"Good grief. What are the names of Mack's brothers?" Her mother held up a hand. "Wait. I don't want to know." She studied Beth. "Are you sure you're friends with Mack, because the look in your eyes when you mention him tells me that you have deeper feelings for him."

"No matter how much I care for Mack, we can never be anything but friends."

"Is it because he didn't go to college?"

"How do you know that?" Beth asked.

"He works at a dude ranch and sings in a country-and-western band."

"You're stereotyping, Mom."

Her mother rolled her eyes. "Why can't you be more than friends with Mack?"

Beth rubbed her finger over the flower pattern on the lunch plate. "You know why."

"I'll say it again…adoption is an option."

Adoption is an option. Adoption is an option. Beth hated her mother's mantra.

"Mack comes from a big family. He has five brothers and a sister and four of them are married with children."

"You've met his family?"

"We took care of his twin nephews when his sister-in-law went into labor."

"How old are the boys?"

"Six." Beth smiled. "One is shy and the other talks your ear off."

"Sounds like you enjoyed being with them."

"I did. But…"

"What, honey?"

"It reminded me all over again that I'll never have children of my own."

"I don't like it when you talk this way. Having a baby doesn't make you a mother. There are lots of women who have babies and give them away or abuse them."

"I've heard all this before from you." Beth shoved her chair back and took her plate to the sink. "I get that I can adopt. I get that thousands of children in this country are waiting to be part of a family." She pressed a hand to her heart. "But it's not the same as looking at the face of a child that's part of you."

"You're right. Adopted children wouldn't look like you, but that doesn't mean they don't become more like you under your care and guidance."

"It doesn't matter. I got the job I interviewed for in San José."

Her mother offered Beth a reprieve and changed the subject. "Tell me about the job."

"Cambridge Financial Investments. They have offices in New York and Chicago, as well as San José." Beth poured herself a glass of water and returned to the table. "And there's an opportunity to advance in the company." An opportunity she hadn't had at Biker and Donavan Investments.

"What's the salary?"

"Twenty thousand more than what I was making in Yuma."

"I'm sorry things didn't work out with Brad but I'll look forward to having you back in California."

Beth summoned a smile. As much as she loved her parents, visiting them wouldn't fill the void in her after she left Mack behind for good.

WEDNESDAY EVENING MACK's boss called him and Hoss to his office for a meeting.

"There's been a change of plans this weekend." Dave's voice sounded garbled in Mack's ears, his thoughts focused solely on Beth, who'd returned to the ranch earlier in the day, supposedly to discuss Dave's financial investments in exchange for him having allowed her to stay at the ranch free of charge. He wanted to know if she got the job in California, but he was still ticked off about the way things had ended between them that he'd resisted the urge to knock on her cabin door and ask.

"Mack, are you on board?" Dave asked.

"Sorry, what was that?"

"The Creighton party from Delaware rescheduled for

next month so with the unexpected vacancy I decided to fulfill a promise I made to a friend."

"What kind of promise?" Hoss asked.

"This Saturday we're hosting a group of kids from the Yuma County Children's Home."

"We got a bunch of ruffians comin' here?" Hoss asked.

"Greg Hansen is the supervisor of the home. He's been bugging me to let him bring the kids to the ranch."

"We can't watch all them kids," Hoss said.

"Since we're shorthanded with Jake gone, Greg is bringing two volunteers with him to help supervise the group."

"How many will there be?" Mack asked.

"I'm not sure. The kids are between the ages of six and fourteen."

"Girls or boys?" Hoss asked.

"Both, I think. Greg didn't offer a whole lot of information about them." Dave crossed his arms behind his head and relaxed in his chair. "Aside from a trail ride in the afternoon before the chuck wagon cookout, any ideas what we can do to entertain these kids?"

"What about a mutton-bustin' rodeo for the younger ones? I can contact P. T. Lewis." The rodeo promoter would know where to find sheep for the event and safety equipment for the little ones.

"I like the idea of keeping the kids in one place," Dave said. "Make it happen. We'll have a mini rodeo before they return to Yuma. We can use it as leverage to make sure they obey the rules." Dave's expression sobered. "The safety of the kids is first and foremost. Is that understood?"

Mack and Hoss nodded.

"And it goes without saying—" Dave nodded to Hoss "—no chewing tobacco in front of them."

Hoss grumbled beneath his breath but didn't object.

"Any questions?" Dave grabbed his notepad. "Okay, let's make sure everyone has fun."

Hoss and Mack left the office—Hoss returning to the barn and Mack staying in the dining room to make a call to P. T. Lewis. The rodeo promoter didn't answer, so he left a message, hoping P.T. would return his call ASAP. If the mutton-bustin' competition fell through, they'd have to come up with a different activity, and kids could only play at roping a pretend steer for so long before they grew bored.

When Mack stepped outside the mess hall, he walked straight to Beth's cabin. So much for being able to ignore her presence. He wouldn't sleep a wink tonight until he found out what had happened with her interview. He knocked twice before she opened the door. Her hair was messy as if he'd woken her from a nap. She looked soft and cuddly, and he wanted to hold her and bury his face in her neck.

"I can't talk right now," she said.

The toe of his boot blocked her attempt to close the door in his face. "How did the job interview go?"

There was a moment's hesitation then she motioned him inside. He remained by the door and she stood behind the chair, arms clasping her waist, looking like a waif. If she'd only used him for a rebound guy, why was she having trouble meeting his gaze? Seconds ticked by, then she spoke. "They offered me the job."

A sharp pain jabbed him in the chest. "Did you accept it?"

"Yes."

He searched for words to express how he felt, but his emotions were a mess and he couldn't think of a damned thing to say. She must have sensed his struggle, because she carried the conversation.

"I stopped to visit my parents." Her gaze flicked to his and in that split second he saw regret in her eyes. Why? Wasn't she happy that she'd landed a new job? Or would she miss him when she left? A sliver of hope worked its way beneath his skin but he was hesitant to make too much of it.

"I hadn't told them about my divorce."

"How did they react?"

"My mother wasn't surprised. My father took it hard. He liked the idea of having a daughter married to a sportscaster."

Mack wondered what Beth's father would say if his daughter married a cowboy musician. "I'm sure your parents want to see you happy." He wanted Beth to be happy, but *he* wanted to be the man who made her happy. "I've thought long and hard about what you told me," he said.

She focused on the floor.

Forget keeping his distance. He crossed the room and grasped her hands, grateful she didn't pull away. "I think you lied to me, Beth Richards."

She stiffened.

"I think I was more than a fling. You know why?"

"Please, Mack. I don't want—"

He held her hand against his heart. "Because the night we made love in Prescott you looked into my eyes and said I made your dreams come true. Remember that?"

Her cheeks turned pink.

"I'm in love with you, Beth." He'd said it first. Put his heart out there for her to stomp on if she chose to. He waited, hoping she'd be honest with him.

"You can't love me," she whispered.

"Give me one good reason why loving you is a bad thing? When I look at you, I see a million ways you make me happy."

She caressed his cheek, the warmth of her touch zapping his heart. "I can't make you happy in the long run."

"You're talking crazy. You already make me happy. And I know I can make you happy." He kissed her temple then her cheek then her mouth. "You watched me sing when you rode the mechanical bull at the bar." He nibbled the side of her neck. "Love, not lust, made your eyes so soft and dark that night."

Tears shimmered on her lashes. "Don't make this any harder than it already is."

"There's nothing difficult about confessing your love for me, Beth. But I can wait until you're ready."

"Stop." She moved away from him and stood across the room. This wasn't going to end the way she hoped, but she owed Mack the truth. "Yes, I love you." *More than I ever thought possible.* The relief that shone in his eyes hurt more than if someone had punched her in the stomach.

"If you love me then you must be imagining a future with me."

Don't ask. "What kind of future do you see for us?"

He grinned. "You go first. I don't want to scare you."

She swallowed hard. "I don't see the same future for us that you see, Mack."

"What do you mean?"

She'd come to terms with never having children,

had even taken a leap of faith by marrying Brad. But her sterility had come back to haunt her, destroying her marriage and sending her down this road of heart-ache with Mack. And for what? Neither of them came out the winner.

"I'm not cut out for motherhood." That was partially true, seeing that she didn't have the necessary biological parts to bear children.

"We haven't discussed having kids, but you know that family is important to me. I've got six siblings and although we bicker and argue, I'm grateful for each and every one of them."

"I know you are. When you're with your family I see how much you care for them."

"Are you worried I'll interfere with your job?" he asked. "I admire you for going to college and earning a degree, and I'll support whatever career choices you make."

The conversation was going too far—he acted as if he'd already proposed and she'd accepted. "Mack, stop."

His eyes widened. "Stop what?"

"Talking about the future, because…" She cringed. "I said I don't want children."

"I know what you said and I can wait—"

"Forever?" Damn him, he was going to make her say it. "Mack, I can't have a baby." Her heart felt as if it might explode. "I'm sterile." The turmoil in his gaze as he digested her words made Beth want to cry.

"Sterile?"

"I developed a severe case of polycystic ovary syndrome in my teens and had to have my ovaries and uterus removed." She waited for him to respond, but in all fairness, what could he say?

The blood drained from his face and without thinking, she hugged him. There was nothing he could say that would change the course of their future. They stood in silence, wrapped in each other's embrace. It took more effort than she expected to let go of him first.

After a few seconds, Mack went to the door, pausing with his hand on the knob.

Please don't say a word. Just go.

Mack granted her wish and left.

Then Beth's heart shattered.

"HI, MACK. C'MON IN. Johnny should be here in a few minutes." Shannon opened the door to her and Johnny's home—the foreman's cabin at the Triple D Ranch—and waved him inside.

He heard a cry from down the hallway. "If you're busy I can check in with Johnny later." He'd thought about calling his brother but had decided against it. He was too confused about his situation with Beth to share his feelings over the phone.

"Don't worry about Addy." Shannon disappeared from the room then reappeared with her daughter on her hip. She wants her daddy." Shannon held out her daughter. "Your uncle Mack will have to do until Daddy walks through the door."

Mack had little choice but to take his niece, and as soon as he settled her against his chest, she stopped fussing and smiled.

"You're a natural with kids, Mack." Shannon went into the kitchen and finished washing the dishes.

The compliment left a hollow feeling inside him. "Addy looks like you, Shannon."

"Maybe, but she's got her father's stubbornness."

Mack swallowed a chuckle. Everyone in the family knew that little Addy was as bullheaded and determined as her mama. It wouldn't surprise him if one day his niece became a better bull rider than Shannon.

The cabin door opened and Johnny walked in. Addy squealed and launched herself toward her father, almost falling out of Mack's arms. Heart pounding, he handed the baby to his brother.

"Hey, Mack. What brings you here in the middle of the week?" Johnny blew loud kisses against Addy's cheeks and the baby squealed.

When Mack glanced toward the kitchen, Johnny said, "Shannon, I'm taking Addy outside for a while."

Mack and Johnny crossed the driveway and entered the barn. Addy began bouncing up and down and waving her arms wildly. "What's she so excited about?"

"She knows I'm gonna put her on the bucking machine." Johnny entered the storage room at the back of the barn and flipped on the lights. As soon as he set his daughter on the machine, she waved her arms wildly.

Holding Addy tight, Johnny flipped the switch and the machine gently swayed. Mack watched father and daughter, his chest tightening at the thought of never having a child of his own with Beth—a little girl the spitting image of her.

"What's the matter, Mack? You look like you're going to be sick."

"Has Porter mentioned anything about a woman who's staying at the guest ranch?" He sat on a storage bin in the corner.

"You mean Beth?"

"He did mention her, then."

"Porter's exact words were that you had the hots for

her." When Mack didn't respond, Johnny asked, "Is it serious between you and this Beth?"

Mack nodded. "I'm in love with her. And she loves me, but…"

"But what?"

Saying it out loud was tougher than he imagined. "She can't have children." He was grateful Johnny didn't spout something stupid just to make him feel better.

"Are you set on having your own kids or is adoption something you'd consider?"

Mack had been in such a state of shock after hearing Beth's confession that adoption never crossed his mind. "I hadn't thought of it."

"If I share something with you, you promise not to tell the others?" Johnny said.

"Sure."

"As much as I loved Grandpa, he was so busy with the orchards he never had time for us kids. I resented him for that. And when Mom came back to the farm expecting another baby, I always hoped she'd marry the man who'd gotten her pregnant because I just wanted a dad. I didn't even care that he wouldn't be my biological father."

"It would have been nice for all of us to have had a father," Mack said. "Someone to throw the baseball with. Talk about girls with. Tear apart a car engine with." If their mother had married any of the men who'd fathered his siblings then they'd all have grown up with a father.

"Look at Conway. He didn't father Mig and Javi, but the boys are loyal to him, and they love him so much. There's no way the twins' real father will ever measure up to Conway or take his place in the boys' hearts."

What Johnny said was true. Mack could have that kind of relationship with a child he adopted.

"Mack?"

He looked at his brother.

"For what it's worth, I think you'd be a great dad whether the kid is yours or not."

"Thanks, Johnny." Now he just had to show Beth that he was okay with adopting.

What if she still says no and insists you deserve to have your own children?

Then he'd have to prove that it was her he couldn't live without, and he didn't want to be a father unless she was by his side helping him raise their son or daughter.

Chapter Thirteen

The minute Mack returned to the dude ranch he headed to Beth's cabin. He'd done all the thinking he'd needed to do, and now he intended to convince the woman of his dreams that together they could have a rich, rewarding life filled with love, laughter and children.

"Mack," Hoss called out as he walked past the barn.

"I'm busy." He lengthened his stride, ignoring the old man's snicker. Beth answered the door after the first knock. He stepped past her, then stopped in the middle of the room.

It took all his concentration to focus on her face and not allow his gaze to wander over her body. "Did you really believe that telling me you can't have children would change the way I feel about you?"

Her eyes watered and his tough-guy attitude crumbled. He closed the distance between them and brushed his thumb over her dewy eyelashes. "I fell in love with you before I knew you couldn't have a baby."

"It doesn't matter how you feel about me, because you're going to eventually want children." The quivering sigh that escaped her lungs squeezed his heart. "You come from a large family and I've seen how much you enjoy being an uncle to Javier and Miguel."

"Marrying you won't stop me from being an uncle."

"One day you'll want your own children."

"You're right, I will."

The color drained from her face, and Mack rushed on. "There are other ways we can have a family, but we don't have to make any decisions—" he spread his arms wide "—before I've even asked you to marry me." Mack read the yearning in Beth's eyes—she wanted the fairy-tale ending he'd dreamed of for them.

"This isn't how I'd planned to propose to you. I haven't even bought you a ring, but it's all I've thought about since we spent the night in Prescott. I've known for a while now that I want to make a life with you." He opened his arms to hug her but she dodged him.

"I can't marry you, Mack. I don't want children. Ever."

"Why not? Lots of good kids need parents."

"You say that now, but you'll change your mind."

"Change my mind about adopting?"

She nodded. "We'll adopt and then you'll decide later that you want a child of your own and…" She sucked in a shuddering breath. "You'll ask for a divorce."

He tamped down his annoyance. "Not all men are like your ex."

"I didn't mean to insult you, it's that—"

"You don't trust me. You don't believe my feelings for you are real and sincere." He shoved a hand through his hair. "I swear, Beth, that my love for you is true blue." A tear dribbled down her cheek, and he hated that he'd made her cry.

"It doesn't matter. You deserve to have the chance to be a father."

"I can have that experience with a child that's not

mine. If you believe it's all biological, then you're denying yourself the opportunity to be all you can be for yourself and others."

She straightened her shoulders. "No, Mack. I won't marry you. You'll thank me later when you hold your own child in your arms."

"And how the hell is that going to happen when I love you?" Feeling his temper give way, Mack decided he had to leave before he said something he couldn't take back. Without a word he walked out the door, leaving it wide open behind him.

"I COUNTED FIFTEEN," Mack said, eyeing the kids who hopped out of the passenger van. He and Hoss stood in the barn doorway.

Hoss squinted at the group. "Glad he brought a couple of babysitters along." Greg Hansen introduced a young man and woman to Dave—probably volunteers at the group home.

"That kid standing off by himself looks like trouble." Mack nodded to a teenage boy. He was taller than the others, and his chin jutted in the air, advertising the big chip on his shoulder.

"The little bean-heads tusslin' with each other seem harmless." Hoss grinned at the kids tugging on each other's clothes.

"The rest appear well behaved," Mack said.

"When's P.T. deliverin' the sheep?"

"Noon. One of us should take a group of kids and get the round pen ready for the sheep. The livestock tank needs water, and hay bales have to be set out."

"I'll do it." Hoss spit tobacco juice at the ground.

Mack nudged the old coot. "The boss said no chewing today."

"Well, hell. I forgot." The geezer pulled the plug of tobacco from his cheek and wrapped it in a handkerchief then stuck it in his pocket. "After we ready the pen, you want me to show 'em my rope tricks?"

"Sounds good." Mack checked his watch. "We've got three hours to entertain them before the trail ride."

"What are you gonna do with the lone teenager?"

"He can help me with the horses in the barn." Mack nodded. "Let's go meet the group."

"Boys and girls, listen up." The supervisor spoke. "This is Mr. Paxton. He owns the Black Jack Mountain Dude Ranch. You do what he says."

"Welcome to the ranch, kids," Dave said. "We've got some fun activities lined up for you, but there are a few rules you need to follow. Those who break the rules will be stuck with me today, and I'm not doing any of the fun stuff." Dave leveled a sober stare at the kids. "Rule number one. No one goes near the horses unless Hoss—" Dave pointed to the old man "—or Mack is with you." Mack waved.

"Rule number two. Don't wander off. Rule number three. Have fun." As soon as Dave mentioned the third rule, the kids erupted into cheers.

Dave signaled Mack to join his side. "Mack is the ranch foreman."

"What's a foreman?" the young girl standing next to Greg asked.

"He's the boss of everyone but me," Dave said. "If he tells you to do something, you do it. If he tells you to stop doing something, you stop."

"If he tells me to jump off a cliff do I gotta do that, too?" Several snickers erupted after the teen's comment.

Mack approached the smart-ass and stood toe-to-toe with the young man, forcing him to crane his neck to maintain eye contact. "What's your name?"

"Ricky."

"I've never had to ask anyone to jump off a cliff, Ricky. Don't make me ask you."

At least the kid had the sense to look nervous. Mack appreciated that the supervisor hadn't intervened and allowed him to deal with Ricky in his own way. "Would anyone else like to challenge my authority before we start the activities?" The kids shook their heads. "Okay, listen up." Mack motioned to the younger ones. "You're going to hang out with Hoss."

Hoss stepped forward. "C'mon, buckaroos. We got work to do if we're gonna have a mutton-bustin' rodeo later on." The boys and girls ran after Hoss, and one of the volunteers joined them.

Mack stuck his finger out again and instructed the rest of the kids to follow Dave, who had set up the steer-roping dummy in another corral. The outspoken teenage boy and one of the girls remained with Greg Hansen.

Mack approached the trio. "Is there a reason she's not going with Hoss and the other kids?"

The brown-haired girl pushed her glasses up her nose and looked at Mack.

"Katy can't participate in any of the activities today. Mutton bustin' and calf roping are off-limits," Hansen said.

Mack wondered why the girl had accompanied the group to the ranch if she wasn't being allowed to join in the fun.

"How about if Katy comes with me?"

Mack spun and came face-to-face with Beth. She must have been standing in the shadows observing everyone. "Beth, this is Katy and the group home supervisor, Greg Hansen."

"Hello, Katy," Beth said then nodded to Hansen.

Obviously not shy, Katy asked, "What are we gonna do, Miss Beth?"

"Do you like to bake?"

"I don't know. I've never baked anything."

"It's easy. I'll show you what to do."

"Okay." Katy reached for Beth's hand, and Mack caught Beth's strained smile as the two walked off.

"What am I supposed to do?" the teen said.

"You're helping me." Mack walked toward the barn, the teen falling in step beside him. "How old are you?"

"Fourteen."

"How long have you been in the home?"

"Long enough."

"Ever take care of a horse before?"

"No."

"Then it's about time you learned how." Mack waited for a sarcastic comeback, but Ricky kept his mouth shut as they entered the barn. "We're taking everyone on a trail ride later."

"You got enough horses for all of us?"

"The little kids are riding in a wagon. You and the adults will be on horseback."

Ricky counted the stalls. "There's only six horses."

"The others are in the pasture."

"I want this one." Ricky stood in front of the first stall.

"That's Potato."

"Dumb name for a horse." Ricky walked over to the next stall. "What about him?"

"Bim Bom's a decent gelding."

"And that one?" The kid pointed farther down the aisle.

"Warrior."

"I get Warrior."

Mack struggled not to smile. Warrior was the slowest horse on the trail, and Mack couldn't remember when he'd moved faster than a trot. "As long as you treat him well, you can ride him." Mack motioned to the supply room. "First you'll need to groom him."

"What's grooming?"

"Brush his coat."

"Why do I have to do that?"

"Shows the horse you respect him and helps him decide if he can trust you." Mack figured the kids in the home didn't have many opportunities to care for animals.

"Does it matter if the horse likes me or not? Doesn't he have to do what I tell him to do?"

Yep, Mack was going to have to keep an eye on this kid. "It matters, because the horse outweighs you by more than a thousand pounds, and if he decides to toss you on your head, he will."

"He doesn't look mean."

"Warrior isn't, but if you mistreat him, he'll fight back." Mack rubbed the horse's neck. "You see that mark on his backside?" He pointed to the scar across the animal's rump.

"Yeah."

"He got that from an abusive owner. It took a long

while for me to gain Warrior's trust after he came to the ranch." Mack stared pointedly at the kid.

"Okay, I get it. Be nice to the horse."

"If you disrespect him, you'll answer to me."

Ricky shot Mack a challenging glare. "So where's the stuff to groom him with?"

Mack retrieved the kit from the storage room and handed Ricky a currycomb. If he thought the teen cared, he'd explain each tool's purpose, but the kid didn't appear interested in listening to anything he had to say.

Once Ricky got the hang of the currycomb, Mack left him alone. Between grooming the other horses and organizing the riding equipment, he managed to walk past the barn opening but never saw Beth and Katy leave the main lodge.

"Who you looking for?" Ricky asked.

"Just making sure none of your friends are getting into trouble."

"We're not bad."

"What do you mean?" Mack asked.

"Everyone thinks just because we live in a group home that we're the worst of the worst and foster parents won't even take us."

Ricky's comment caught Mack's attention. "You're saying that you're not as tough as you want everyone to believe?"

Ricky shrugged. "I'm tough, but I'm not mean."

"I believe you." Mack nodded to the tack room. "C'mon. I'll show you what you need to saddle a horse in case you decide to be a cowboy one day."

"Why would I want to be a cowboy?" Ricky dogged Mack's boot heels.

"You ever been to a rodeo?"

"What's so special about rodeo?"

"It's exciting, and you seem like the kind of guy who loves a physical challenge. You're too big for mutton bustin' but maybe we can find you a small steer to ride later today." Mack chuckled. "You can decide if getting bucked off is worth the thrill of the ride."

Ricky smiled. "Wanna bet I can hang on?"

"Sure. If you fall off, I get your dessert."

"And if I don't, you have to take me to a rodeo."

The yearning for a male role model shone bright in Ricky's eyes, and Mack felt bad that the kid didn't have a family. "Okay. If you stay on the steer, we'll go to a rodeo."

"How old are you?"

Beth was taken aback by Katy's question as they entered the main building that housed the ranch kitchen. "Don't you know you're not supposed to ask another lady's age?"

"Why?" Katy's big brown eyes widened. "I tell everyone I'm ten years old."

"Most ladies don't like growing old. That's why we keep our age a secret." Beth forced herself to relax in the little girl's presence. She hadn't gotten a wink of sleep since Mack had asked her to marry him, and she'd turned him down flat. Even now when she recalled the frustrated expression on his face as he stormed from her cabin, she believed with all her heart she'd done the right thing. She loved Mack—enough to let him go. She just didn't expect it to hurt this badly.

"José?" she called out before entering the kitchen. He stepped from the pantry. "Katy and I would like to bake cookies if we won't be in your way." José flipped through the pages of a cookbook before pointing to a recipe, then he left the room.

"Do you like chocolate-chip cookies?"

"I like any kind of cookies," Katy said.

"Chocolate chip, it is." Beth rummaged in the cupboards, setting out mixing bowls, baking sheets and measuring spoons and cups. "What temperature does it say to preheat the oven, Katy?"

The little girl squinted at the recipe book. Beth helped her out, indicating the temperature. "Three-fifty."

After setting the oven temperature, Beth browsed the pantry shelves. "What if I read the recipe and you put the ingredients into the bowl?"

Katy dragged a chair to the counter and stood on the seat. "What do you want me to do first?"

"We need to decide how many cookies to make."

"A lot."

"We'll triple the recipe. That means six eggs go in this bowl." She set the largest mixing bowl in front of Katy. "Get cracking."

Katy frowned. "How do I crack an egg?"

Beth thought it odd that a child Katy's age had never cracked open an egg, but maybe the cook in the group home didn't allow kids in the kitchen. Beth cracked the first egg and handed the next one to Katy. "How many girls are in the home with you?"

"Sally, Amber, Crystal, Cassy and Jennifer. They're older than me and they're not very nice."

"Good job," Beth said, after Katy finished with the eggs. She didn't like hearing that Katy might be bullied at the home. She held out a measuring cup. "Six cups of sugar."

"The other girls don't like me." Katy dumped the sugar into the bowl.

Before she realized her actions, Beth tucked a strand of hair behind Katy's ear.

"Jennifer calls me an ugly duckling."

Beth's heart tumbled. Katy wasn't a beautiful little girl, but she had big brown eyes and a nice smile. "Maybe they're jealous of you and don't want you to know it." She pushed the flour bag closer. "Eight cups of flour." When Katy grew quiet, Beth asked, "What happened to your family?"

"I don't know. Mrs. Beanker says I was—"

"Who is Mrs. Beanker?"

"She's the lady trying to find me a family." Mrs. Beanker must be the social worker assigned to Katy's case.

"She said my mom died when I was a baby, and she doesn't know who my dad is."

"I guess your mother didn't have any family," Beth said.

Katy shrugged.

"Have you ever lived with another family?"

"Mrs. Beanker says I had lots of families when I was a baby." Katy set the measuring cup on the counter. "Now what?"

Beth handed her the measuring spoons. "Three tablespoons of vanilla."

"Which one is the tablespoon?"

"The biggest one."

After Katy added the vanilla flavoring into the mix,

she set down the bottle of vanilla and hugged Beth. "Thank you."

Beth couldn't halt the tender feeling spreading through her and hugged Katy back. "They're just cookies."

"Not for the cookies," Katy mumbled against the front of Beth's blouse. "Thank you for being nice to me."

Tears burned Beth's eyes but she held them at bay. A little girl shouldn't have to thank an adult for being nice.

"I hope Mrs. Beanker finds me a mom just like you."

Beth extricated herself from Katy's hug. "Honey, I'm not a mom. I don't have any children."

"Don't you like kids?"

Beth didn't answer the question. Instead, she hooked up an electric mixer, then flipped it to low and combined the ingredients. When she finished she handed a beater to Katy and kept one for herself. "This is the best part of making cookies."

After Katy licked the beater clean, she asked, "Can I dump the bags of chocolate into the bowl?"

"Sure."

"This is hard," Katy said, trying to stir the chips.

"Want me to help?"

"I can do it." When chocolate morsels flew across the counter, Katy quit stirring.

"What's the matter?"

"I'm making a mess."

"So?"

"Aren't you gonna get mad at me?"

"Of course not."

Katy's mouth widened into a huge smile that made

her eyes sparkle, and Beth saw the true beauty in the child.

"I wish you were my mom."

A sharp pain stabbed Beth in the chest. "Someday Mrs. Beanker is going to find you a very nice mom and dad."

"No, she's not."

"Why do you say that?"

"She said I cost too much money."

"That's absurd," Beth said. "How can a little girl like you cost too much money?"

Katy set aside the spoon and lifted her T-shirt, exposing her bony chest—a chest with a thick, pink scar running down the center of it. "I have a sick heart."

The blood drained from Beth's head. "How sick?"

"Mrs. Beanker said I got a brand-new heart from a little boy who died in a car accident."

"When did you get your new heart?"

She held up two fingers.

"Two years ago?"

"When I was two years old. I don't remember it."

"And your heart has worked well ever since?" Beth asked.

"Yeah, but I can't do the stuff other kids do."

"Like what?"

"I can't run, and I'm not supposed to play sports or games on the playground 'cause I could get bumped in the chest." Katy stuck her finger into the dough then licked it. "I have to watch the other kids play."

"How often do you see a doctor to have your heart checked?"

"A lot. And I have to take a lot of pills to keep my heart healthy."

"I think we're ready to put the cookie dough on the baking sheets." With a smaller spoon Beth showed Katy the amount of dough to use for each cookie. They worked in silence and once they finished, Beth slid the cookies into the oven. "Now we wait twelve minutes."

"I'm bored," Katy said.

Beth laughed, making light of the moment, but also acknowledging how often a little girl with a severe heart condition must suffer from boredom when her activities were restricted. "Do you like to read?"

"I'm not very good."

"Are there books to read at the home where you live?"

"Yeah, but I don't read them."

"Why not?"

"It hurts my eyes."

"Did you tell Mrs. Beanker it hurts your eyes?"

Katy nodded. "She said I can't get new glasses until next year, 'cause there's not enough money. My heart medicine costs too much."

Beth wondered about the kind of health care Katy received living in a group home. Her medical bills must be astronomical. Then Beth considered the comfortable income she made and she was ashamed that she'd chosen to wallow in self-pity rather than embrace the opportunity to fulfill her dream of motherhood in a different way. Ashamed that she'd let her fears keep her from reaching out for her own happiness.

And it took a ten-year-old girl with a heart condition to make her see the light. "I hope you know how special you are, Katy."

"I'm not special."

"Oh, yes, you are." Beth hugged her. "You're more special than you'll ever know."

So special I want to keep you for myself.

Chapter Fourteen

"Do you think Ricky will stay on?" Beth stood next to Mack outside the round pen where the kids had gathered to watch the teen ride.

"We'll see. He's nervous." Mack breathed in Beth's scent—a subtle combination of warm woman and faded perfume. After Hoss gave Ricky last-minute instructions, Mack asked, "How did things go with Katy?"

"She's a sweet girl."

Mack heard the strain in her voice and tried to read between the lines. He assumed it had been difficult for Beth to be with the little girl, knowing she'd never be able to—make that never allow herself to—have a daughter of her own. Mack wished with all his heart that he could fix Beth's body so she could have a baby, but even more he wished he could make her understand that her sterility wouldn't stop him from loving her.

Damn her cheating ex—Mack sympathized with Beth's fear of a man leaving her again and wished he knew how to make her believe that he wasn't the lovin' and leavin' kind and that his love for her was unconditional. "What did you ladies chat about?"

"Katy's been in foster care most of her life."

"Too bad they can't find these kids permanent homes."

"In Katy's case I think it might be because of her heart condition," Beth said.

"What heart condition?"

"She had a heart transplant when she was two."

Wow. "Where are her biological parents?"

"Her mother died after Katy was born and according to Katy, the case worker doesn't know the identity of her father." A heartfelt sigh escaped Beth, and Mack sensed the little girl's situation touched her deeply.

"Because of her heart condition I'm sure her medical bills are steep. That's got to be the reason they can't find her a home," Beth said.

"Why do you say that?"

"She such a sweet girl. She'd be easy to love."

Beth had already fallen under Katy's spell.

"The older girls at the home make fun of her. Kids can be so cruel."

Beth was acting like a mama bear toward a child she'd met only a few hours ago. How could she deny herself the experience of being a mother when she was obviously cut out to be one?

"A lot of kids are cruel when they're young." Hell, even adults were cruel—grown men taunted Mack about his name.

"Looks like Ricky's ready to ride. I'm going to watch from the stands." Beth took two steps then stopped. "Mack?"

"Yeah?"

"I'm leaving on Monday for San José."

His heart plunged into his stomach. "When does the new job start?"

"In three weeks." She walked off as if dropping bombshells was an everyday habit of hers.

Beth might be leaving the ranch but that didn't mean Mack was giving up on her. Or them. He moved closer to the chute where Hoss had loaded the steer. "You ready, kid?"

Ricky's voice shook. "I can do this."

"Yes, you can. Scoot forward a bit. That's it. Lean back. Not too much. Right there. Now, as soon as Hoss hits the steer's rump and scares him out of the chute, he's gonna kick with his back legs and that will push you forward, so hang on tight."

"How do I get off when I'm done?"

Mack ignored Hoss's grin. "Don't worry about the dismount, the steer will take care of that for you. When you're ready, you nod once and that's the signal for Hoss to open the gate."

Ricky sat for a few seconds, clasping and unclasping his fingers around the rope. Sweat broke out across his brow, and Mack hoped the kid didn't back down. Whether the teen believed it or not, he needed to prove to himself that he had the courage to see this ride through to the end.

Ricky nodded, and Hoss opened the gate then smacked the steer's rump, and the animal bolted into the corral. The steer spun and kicked out in an attempt to unload the weight on its back, but Ricky hung on—his body jerking with the steer's wild gyrations. Mack studied Ricky's face—his narrow-eyed squint showed focus and determination. With a few lessons and a lot of practice, he'd be a great candidate for a junior rodeo career.

And who's going to help him practice when he's stuck in a group home?

Mack didn't have time to contemplate the question when Hoss clanged the cowbell, signaling that Ricky had ridden eight seconds. Mack hopped into the corral ready to intervene once Ricky launched himself off the steer. "Jump into the spin!"

The teen dove off, hit the ground and rolled. "Nice ride," Mack said. He guided the steer to the opposite side of the corral and removed the flank strap.

Ricky approached Mack. "When are we gonna go to that rodeo you promised me?" The kid grinned and Mack swore he saw the chip fall off the boy's shoulder.

"There's a rodeo in Sierra Vista next month. We'll go to that one."

"Isn't there one sooner?" The teen was clearly worried Mack would forget.

"It's only a few weekends away."

"Yeah, whatever." Ricky walked off and joined the rest of the kids who high-fived him.

Beth and Katy sat together, the little girl chatting nonstop with her hand resting on Beth's leg. Then Beth laughed at something Katy said and he smiled at the sweet picture the pair made. No one would guess that the two weren't mother and daughter. He switched his focus to Ricky. There was so much potential in the teen. With the right guidance and a little attention he'd grow into a fine young man.

Ricky and Katy need a family.

Hoss shouted orders to prepare the sheep for the mutton-bustin' competition, but Mack blocked out the commotion, his mind churning with an idea that scared the hell out of him and excited him all at once. It might possibly be the most important decision he made in his life, but as he watched Beth, he came to the conclusion that it was a decision he couldn't afford not to make.

"WE'RE ALL HERE," Johnny said, taking a seat at the table in the bunkhouse.

Mack had requested the family meeting, and the entire Cash clan had crowded into the bunkhouse Wednesday night—even Buck and Destiny had made the drive from Lizard Gulch with their two-week-old son, Cody. Mack's heart swelled with love and gratitude for his expanding family.

Conway's twin daughters, Emma and Molly, fussed in their parents' arms. Javi and Mig were sprawled on the carpet, wrestling with Bandit. Dixie held a sleeping Nate in her lap. Shannon bounced a bright-eyed Addy on her knee and the tyke squealed.

Mack grinned. "If there was ever a girl born to ride bulls, it's Addy."

"Tell me about it," Johnny grumbled.

Shannon nodded to Will and Marsha's son. "That's why I've given Ryan the task of improving protective gear for women roughstock riders."

"Aunt Shannon says the Kevlar vest she had to wear was too heavy for her," Ryan said. "I'm researching different materials to use in the future."

Shannon beamed at her nephew. "When Addy is old enough to ride, Ryan will have figured it out."

"Where's Beth?" Johnny asked. "Why isn't she here?"

"She's in California." Not for long—Mack hoped. "I asked everybody here today because I've made a big decision in my life and I need your help." Especially if Beth declined his marriage proposal.

"This sounds serious," Dixie said.

Suspecting his siblings would believe he'd lost his mind, Mack took a deep breath and said, "I'm going to adopt two kids. A fourteen-year-old boy and a ten-year-old girl."

Dead silence echoed through the bunkhouse. "I met the kids last week when they came to the dude ranch. They live in a group home in Yuma and both of them have been in foster care most of their lives."

"But you're not married," Dixie said.

Mack intended to propose to Beth, but he didn't want to risk her believing that he'd only asked her to marry him because he needed a mother for the kids—that's why he'd already begun the adoption process. Whether Beth agreed to marry him or not, he intended to become Ricky and Katy's father.

"I'm asking for your help in raising these kids. I don't know anything about being a father—" he made eye contact with each of his married brothers "—but I've watched all of you with your own kids and I see how happy you are and how fulfilling your lives have become.... I want that, too."

"You could get married and have your own children," Will said.

Mack met Johnny's gaze. His brother knew the woman Mack loved couldn't have children, and he refused to marry someone else just so he could father his own kids. "Ricky and Katy need me and I want us to be a family."

"What about your job?" Porter asked. "And the band?"

"As far as the band goes, we'll get together once in a while for a gig, but I'm ready to move on from that part of my life. I've decided to search for a townhouse in Yuma so the kids are close to their schools."

"That's over an hour commute to the dude ranch," Johnny said.

"I realize that, but I want Ricky and Katy to be able to participate in after-school activities."

"Since Gavin and I live in Yuma," Dixie said, "I can pick up the kids after school and bring them to my shop. They're welcome to eat dinner with us if you have to work late."

Mack's chest tightened. He didn't think he could love his baby sister any more than he did right at that moment.

"When I get my driver's license, Uncle Mack," Ryan said, "I can help out on weekends when you're at the ranch."

"They can always ride the bus home with Ryan to Stagecoach and do their schoolwork at our house until you pick them up," Will said.

Mack grinned. "I knew I could count on you all."

"So when do we get to meet the kids?" Johnny asked.

"Their case worker wants to talk with you first, Johnny."

The eldest Cash brother nodded. "I'll meet him or her anytime anywhere."

"I appreciate that. The paperwork takes a while, so I'll be their foster parent for several months until the judge sets a court date for the adoption hearing. Once I find a place with separate bedrooms for the kids, we can all live together while we wait for the adoption to be finalized."

Conway's wife, Isi, cleared her throat. "I'd like to know when Porter is going to settle down."

Porter's eyes widened. "Why me?"

"Because you're too much fun. Javi and Mig would rather play with you than do their chores or homework."

"Hey, there's no such thing as too much fun. Besides—" Porter pointed at Mack "—now that he won't be living in the bunkhouse, Javi and Mig can move in with me."

"Yeah!" Mig shouted.

"I like Uncle Porter," Javi said. "He lets us eat all the Skittles after his poker game."

Porter cleared his throat loudly and the twins stopped talking.

"I think kicking my brothers out and making them move into the bunkhouse has been the best thing ever," Dixie said.

"Why's that?" Shannon asked.

"It's forced them all to grow up."

The brothers groaned, and Isi waggled her finger at Porter. "Five brothers down, one to go."

Right then little Cody woke and began wailing, which startled Emma and Molly, and they joined in the crying. Then Nate whined—so much for peace and quiet. Mack grinned at each of his brothers. He was a lucky guy. He had six awesome siblings, and he was about to get his own family. All he had to do was make Beth see that she didn't want to miss out on all the happiness that awaited her if she chose to spend the rest of her life with him.

"Mr. Hansen, I don't know if you remember me—"

"Sure, I do." The supervisor of the Yuma group home

for children greeted Beth. "You can call me Greg if I can call you Beth." He waved at a chair in front of his desk, and Beth sat down. "Katy hasn't stopped talking about you since she visited the dude ranch."

"I hope you don't mind me dropping by without an appointment."

"Now is the best time to chat since the kids are in school." He glanced at the wall clock. "In a few hours they'll get off the bus and this place will be chaos until lights out." He leaned back in his chair. "What can I do for you?"

Beth's pulse raced. She was so sure she'd thought through her idea, but now that she was here she worried if she was doing the right thing. Her heart said yes, but she feared she might not be good enough for what she was about to ask. Taking a deep breath she said, "I'd like to inquire about the process of adopting Katy."

"Have you ever been a foster parent?"

"No. And I understand that this is coming out of the blue, but I felt a special connection to Katy and…" *I'm ready to try— No.* "I'm ready to be a mother."

"You're not married, are you?"

"No, I'm divorced. Is that a problem?"

"We like to place kids in a two-parent home, but in Katy's case that probably won't ever happen."

"She told me about her medical condition," Beth said. "I realize she'll need a doctor's care for the rest of her life, and that there will be ongoing expenses. I recently accepted a job with a San José investment firm, and I'll have medical coverage for both of us. My salary will more than cover our living expenses and Katy's care."

"So you'd want to take Katy to California to live."

"Actually, I'll be staying in Yuma. I've made arrangements with my employer to work from home. Once a month I'll need to fly to California for meetings, but I'll arrange for Katy's care while I'm gone. Is that a problem?"

"It sounds like you've thought this through, but I'm sorry to say that we've found a foster home for Katy, and the foster parent has expressed interest in adopting her, too." Greg shook his head. "All these years and no one's reached out to Katy, then suddenly there are two people who want her."

Beth's ears buzzed. Of all the scenarios she imagined, this one had never entered her mind.

"I'll tell you what, Beth. If Katy has any trouble adjusting to her new foster home, I'll be in touch."

Feeling numb, Beth stood. "Katy's happiness—" not hers "—is what matters most." Eyes burning, she left the home and got into her car then willed herself not to cry. *Go figure.* She finally allowed herself to dream of being a mother and all her bravery had gotten her was more rejection.

What about Mack?

He was the reason she'd gone to the children's home today. His faith in her had given her the courage to accept the truth—that she did want to be a mother and no matter how much the responsibility scared her, she believed as Mack had that she'd make a great mom.

So are you going to listen to your heart again and admit that you're in love with Mack?

She started the engine and drove south toward the dude ranch. She wanted to be a mother. Wanted to have a family. Most of all she wanted Mack. Without him by her side nothing else mattered.

What if he's changed his mind about marrying you?
Then she'd just have to change it back.

"BETH, WHAT A SURPRISE," Dave said when she entered his office at the dude ranch.

"I'm probably the last person you expected to see again."

Dave frowned. "Didn't the job in California work out?"

"The job's great. I was hoping to speak with Mack, but I didn't see his truck parked outside."

"He's in Yuma on business, but he should return shortly. Why don't you wait for him in the cantina and help yourself to the iced tea while you're there."

"When Mack gets back, will you tell him—"

"Of course, Beth."

A fire blazed in the cantina fireplace, lending the room a cozy feel. She was too nervous to sit, so she paced the floor, stopping at the front window, hoping to catch a glimpse of Mack's truck. She had no idea what she'd say to him except *I love you.*

She waited for almost an hour when she spotted a vehicle approach on the ranch road. *Mack.* As the pickup drew closer, she spied someone sitting in the passenger seat. He parked in front of the office and got out. Beth's heart tumbled at the sight of him. Lord, she hoped he'd give her a second chance.

The passenger door opened and she gasped. *Ricky?* What was he doing with Mack? Her heart stopped beating altogether when Katy hopped out of the backseat. *What in the world?* Beth dashed out the door and cut across the parking lot.

"Miss Beth!" Katy called out, running toward her.

Beth opened her arms and hugged the little girl close. "I missed you, Miss Beth."

"I've missed you, too, Katy."

Mack, who'd stopped a few feet away, stared at her with a sober expression. "Ricky, before you work on your riding lessons take Katy inside and ask José if he has any donuts leftover from breakfast."

When the kids disappeared, Beth spoke. "It's nice of you to give them riding lessons."

Mack hadn't expected to find Beth at the ranch. He'd brought Ricky and Katy out here for the day because he had to check on the cattle, and Hoss said he'd give the kids horseback lessons to keep them busy until Mack finished his chores. Then after he returned the kids to the home in Yuma, he was meeting a Realtor to view rental properties. He'd wanted to find a place to live before he contacted Beth—so she'd know he was serious about being the kids' father. Her eyes glistened with tears and he grasped her arms. "What's the matter?"

"Just about everything." She waved toward the main building the kids had gone into. "Did you hear that someone's going to adopt Katy?"

Startled that she knew, he asked, "How did you find out?"

"I spoke with Greg yesterday. I wanted to check on Katy and see if…" Her voice wobbled.

He tipped her chin, the sorrow in her eyes breaking his heart. "See if what?"

"Mack, please tell me it's not too late for us," she whispered.

His heart stopped beating, then resumed with a fierce pounding.

She brushed at her wet eyes. "I'm stubborn and it

took me a while to admit that what I want. What makes me happy… What brings joy to me is you."

Mack thought his heart would explode inside his chest.

"I met with Greg to inquire about adopting Katy, but someone had already taken her in. I wanted to prove to you that I was ready to be a mother, because I know how much family means to you." She sucked in a shuddering breath. "I was hoping you and I could adopt Katy and be a family." Tears rolled down her cheeks. "I'm happy Katy's going to get the family she's always wanted, but I wish it could have been us."

"She doesn't have a complete family yet, Beth."

"What do you mean?"

Mack held Beth's face in his hands. "Your tears are killing me. Can I kiss you?"

She nodded.

Mack brushed his lips across hers, tasting her salty tears. That she wanted to show him she could be a mother by adopting Katy humbled him. When he pulled back, he said, "Katy still needs a mother. And so does Ricky."

This was the craziest second attempt at a marriage proposal he could have imagined. No candlelit dinner, no romantic music, no dimmed lights. "I'm Katy and Ricky's foster father."

Beth gasped.

"Wait here." He returned to the truck and rummaged through the glove compartment until he found the jeweler's box, then returned to Beth. "Whether or not I was able to become Ricky or Katy's foster father, I'd planned to ask you to marry me. Again." He opened the lid of the box. "This ring belonged to Grandma Ada."

Beth's eyes rounded.

"My grandmother didn't give birth to her seven grandchildren, but she was more of a mother to us than our real mother could have ever hoped to be. She not only took care of us, she nurtured us and made us feel loved and important. And she taught us kids the real meaning of family. I can't think of anyone better suited to carry on Grandma Ada's love for family than you." He went down on one knee. "Beth, will you marry me?"

Her smile wobbled. "Yes, Mack. I'd be honored to be your wife."

He pushed the ring over her finger, surprised at how well it fit. "I love you, Beth." He stood then pulled her into his arms and kissed her tenderly.

"I know you have a job in California, but we'll make it work, because there's no way I'm letting you go."

"Were you that certain I'd marry you?" she asked.

"I was scared to death you'd say no, but I wanted to show you that I was okay with not having kids of my own." He shrugged. "I knew you had a soft spot for Katy, and I see a lot of potential in Ricky. He's a good kid who just needs to know someone gives a damn about him. Together we can give both kids a loving home."

"If I had said no to your proposal, would you still have gone through with adopting them?"

"Of course. My siblings agreed to help me out with the kids."

"I love you, Mack Cash. You're an amazing man, and I'm glad I had a one-night stand with you." She giggled. "I never thought I'd say this, but I'm thankful Brad cheated on me, or I never would have found you and never would have had a family of my own to love and cherish."

"I'm looking at properties with a Realtor this afternoon. If you're going to be living with us a few days a month, then you should have a say where we live."

"What do you mean a few days a month?"

"You're working in San José, right? That means you'll be commuting home on the weekends."

"My employer hired me as a contractor for the firm. That way I can work from home and travel to California for meetings as needed."

"Hey, Mr. Mack," Ricky called out as he walked toward them, Katy trailing behind. "José said we can stay for supper." Ricky noticed Mack's hand resting on Beth's waist. "What's up with you guys? Are you like girlfriend and boyfriend?"

"Right now we're fiancée and fiancé," Beth said.

"What's a fiancée?" Katy asked.

"Beth and I are getting married," Mack said.

The little girl's mouth dropped open.

"Seriously?" Ricky gaped.

"Seriously."

Katy grasped Beth's hand. "Does this mean you're gonna be my mom?"

"Yes, it does." She glanced at Ricky. "And I'd like to be your mother, Ricky. If that's okay with you?"

The teen shrugged. "Sure. I guess."

Katy clapped her hands. "Yeah! We're gonna be a real family." She hugged Ricky. "And you're gonna be my big brother."

"I guess that means I'm stuck with you for a little sister." Ricky smiled at Katy.

"I think the four of us are going to make a great family," Mack said.

"When are you guys gonna get married?" Ricky asked.

Mack nodded to Beth—no way was he answering that question. Weddings were a woman's business. He'd make sure to show up whenever and wherever Beth wanted.

"How about right away?" Beth said.

"Cool," Ricky said.

Katy hugged Beth.

"What about a big wedding and all the trimmings?" Mack asked.

"I'd rather get married by the justice of the peace with Katy and Ricky as our witnesses. I don't want to wait any longer to become a family."

"Sounds good to me." More than good. Mack listened to Katy pepper Beth with questions, then Ricky began asking Mack about rodeo and pretty soon both kids were talking at once, their voices animated, their eyes bright.

Mack was the luckiest man on earth. "Before we get carried away making plans for the future, I have some news for you two." He eyed the kids.

"What kind of news?" Ricky asked.

"The four of us are going to be a family but we're also going to become part of a bigger family."

"Mack has five brothers and one sister," Beth said. "You'll have a lot of cousins."

"Anyone my age?" Ricky asked.

"My brother Will has a son who'll be sixteen soon. Ryan's the closest to you in age."

"Cool," Ricky said.

"Are there any girls?" Katy asked.

"Three," Mack said, "but they're all babies."

"I like babies."

"And you'll have a grandmother and grandfather," Beth said, hugging Mack.

As Beth told the kids about their grandparents in San Diego and that they'd take a trip to meet them soon, and would definitely have to stop at Disneyland along the way, Mack's throat swelled with emotion. If someone had told him a year ago that he'd find his soul mate and become a father all within a few months, he would have accused them of being crazy.

Now he was thinking he might be the crazy one. But crazy was good, and there was nowhere else he'd rather be right now than crazy in love with Beth and crazy happy about his new family.

Epilogue

"Ladies and gentlemen, are you ready to kick off the Blythe Stampede Rodeo's junior division bull-riding event?"

The handful of fans sitting in the stands hooted and hollered. A group of young girls held up posters with the names of local junior cowboys and big pink hearts painted on them.

"Didn't Ricky decide to ride in the bronc competition today?" Beth asked as she and Mack watched their son put on his Kevlar vest and riding glove—next to a chute with a bull inside. Surrounded by Cash males and former lady-bull-rider Shannon, Beth only caught glimpses of her son's head in the crowd. She hadn't gotten a wink of sleep last night, fretting about today and hoping nothing would go wrong with Ricky's ride. It didn't matter if he won or lost today—she just wanted him to stay safe.

"Hoss has been sharing stories about his bull-riding days with Ricky," Mack said. "And remember the sleepover he had at Ryan's house a while back?" Beth nodded. "Will took the boys out to the Triple D, and Shannon let them get on the bucking machine. Ryan didn't care for it, but Ricky got hooked so Shannon gave him a few lessons."

"And Ricky decided he liked bulls better than broncs."

"Looks that way." Mack pulled Beth close, and she soaked in his comfort. "Don't worry, mama bear, your cub will be fine."

She'd have to trust Mack on this one. She knew next to nothing about rodeo or motherhood, and she was learning along the way. As she took in the action, an ache that had become all too common lately spread through her body—a happy ache and one she prayed would never go away. So far, motherhood had been a fascinating, joyous experience, and each morning she woke wondering what the day had in store for her and her new family. She and Mack, with Ricky and Katy, had settled into a routine as a family, and a stranger would be hard-pressed to guess that the four of them had only just met a few months ago.

"Mom!"

Beth's gaze flew to her son sitting on the junior-sized bull in the chute. Ricky had begun calling her mom a few weeks ago and when he used the moniker, her heart swelled with love. Katy had called her mom before the adoption papers had been signed, but Ricky hadn't given his trust as easily. He still used Mack's first name, but Beth was certain that eventually he'd learn, as she had, that Mack was true blue.

"Smile, Mom." Ricky grinned. "It's gonna be okay."

She gave him a thumbs-up. She was learning that *worry* was a big part of motherhood—she just hadn't expected it to consume her daily routine.

"You sure you don't want to watch in the stands with Katy and your parents?" Mack asked.

"I'm staying." She wanted to show Ricky that she supported him, but mostly she needed to remain close by so that if anything happened... "Katy will be fine. She's helping Dixie entertain Nate." Beth glanced toward the seating section where the Cash wives sat with their babies and her parents right next to them.

The Cash family had opened their hearts to her, Ricky and Katy, and Beth felt truly blessed that her children would grow up surrounded by a large family and lots of love. And Beth had yet to figure out how Mack had won over her father, who now bragged to his golf buddies about his famous rock-star-cowboy son-in-law. As for her mother—she broke down in tears when Beth told her she and Mack were adopting two children. Beth hadn't realized how her inability to have children had weighed heavily on her mother's heart all these years. Now her mother was embracing her role as a grandparent and had insisted on purchasing Katy's new eyeglasses—a designer pair no less—and a new wardrobe for the little girl. Beth's father had given Ricky a beginner's set of golf clubs, but she wasn't sure the clubs would be used...for a few years, anyway.

"Let's move closer so we have a better view." Mack grasped Beth's hand and they approached the chute. "Ricky, listen to Shannon," Mack said. "She's the best bull rider in the family."

"I know. Aunt Shannon told me what to do."

Not a day went by that Mack didn't surprise Beth. His respect for his sister-in-law's talent in a male-dominated sport convinced her that they were going to raise a young man who respected women and a daughter who wouldn't be afraid to chase her dreams despite her physical limitations.

"You can do it, dude." Ryan gave his cousin a fist pump.

"Go get 'em, Ricky!" Beth shouted, squeezing Mack's hand.

"Up first today is Ricky Cash, a fifteen-year-old buckaroo from Yuma, Arizona."

The sparse crowd gathered inside the arena applauded.

"This is Ricky's first time competing. Let's see how this young man does on Thunder Mountain, a junior bull from the famed Valley Springs Ranch in Silver City, New Mexico."

Before Beth was prepared, the chute opened and the bull sprang forward. She held her breath—watching Ricky's torso jerk as the bull's bucking flung him every which way. Resisting the urge to close her eyes, she recited a litany of prayers in her head. She'd made a promise to herself when she became Ricky and Katy's mother that she would embrace every aspect of motherhood—the good, the bad and the scary.

The bull spun, and Ricky slid sideways on the animal's back, but he managed to regain his balance and straighten up right before the bull executed another high buck just as the buzzer sounded. Beth clutched Mack's arm, praying for a safe dismount. Ricky launched himself off the bull and dove for the ground, hitting the dirt hard. He rolled away from the bull's hind legs and scrambled to his feet as the rodeo helpers moved in and guided the bull out of the arena.

Now that the danger was over, Beth's heartbeat returned to normal—for all of five seconds. Was it the arena lighting or did Ricky's face look pale? He walked over to the cowboy hat Beth's father had purchased for his fifteenth birthday and picked it up slowly. Something was wrong. Beth made a move to meet Ricky when he stepped into the cowboy ready area but Mack held her arm. "Give him a minute to bask in the glory."

"Dude, you were awesome!" Ryan playfully punched Ricky in the shoulder, and Beth caught his wince. She suspected her son was a little bruised and sore from the ride and dismount.

After a few more congratulations, Beth decided she'd waited long enough and pushed through the group. "Honey, you were amazing." Beth had begun calling the kids *honey* right after they moved into the new townhouse in Yuma in March. When she offered him a hug, he whispered in her ear.

"Mom, I think I broke my wrist."

She sucked in a quiet breath.

"Don't say anything," he said. "Aunt Shannon will feel bad and I don't want Mack to be disappointed if I can't ride in the finals."

"Your father won't be disappointed, Ricky." Tamping down the panic building inside her she said, "Let's go to the first-aid station and have them take a look at your wrist." She waved to Mack. "We'll be right back."

"I think I broke it on the dismount," Ricky said. "I felt a sharp pain go up my arm, and then when I tried to move my wrist it really hurt."

"Is your wrist the only thing that hurts?"

He grinned. "Heck, no. I ache all over."

"Honey, are you sure you—"

"Mom, I know what you're going to say. I know I

don't have to rodeo just because Mack and my uncles rodeo."

"Don't forget your Aunt Shannon."

"And my aunt. But this is the first time I've been given a chance to test myself and see what I can do. I don't know if I'll ever be as good at rodeo as the rest of the family but I want to try."

"Even if it means a few more broken bones?" she asked.

"I can handle broken bones." He stopped walking and faced Beth. "I want to make it hard for people to guess that I'm not your real son."

"But you are my real son, Ricky."

"You know what I mean. I want people to think I've always been a Cash."

Beth's heart ached for him and the years he'd lived in foster care and group homes, always wondering where he belonged. "I'll support you if you make me a promise."

"What kind of promise?"

"That you believe no matter what you do with your life—no matter what direction your interests lead you—that you'll be true to yourself and know that your happiness is all I and your father want for you."

"That's a promise I can make, Mom."

"I'm going to hold you to it, young man."

When they arrived at the first-aid station, the paramedic took all of fifteen seconds to examine Ricky's wrist before giving his diagnosis—broken. He advised Beth to take Ricky to an orthopedic doctor and get the bone X-rayed, then he wrapped Ricky's wrist in an elastic bandage and gave him an ice bag to help with the swelling.

"Are you mad?" Ricky asked as they walked to the stands.

"I'm not mad, honey, just worried. I hate to see you in pain."

Ricky stopped walking. "You're not gonna make me quit rodeo, are you?"

"Of course not." She smiled. "But you're not going to expect me to stop worrying, are you?"

Ricky laid his uninjured arm across her shoulders. "I'm glad you worry about me."

"Be careful what you wish for."

"No one's ever cared what's happened to me before," he said.

"Now you have a huge family that cares." They arrived at their seating section. When Mack looked their way and spotted the ice bag on Ricky's arm he rushed over, the rest of the family following.

"How bad is it?" Mack asked Ricky.

"Mom, you tell him."

"The paramedic thinks he broke his wrist. We'll have to see a doctor to have it X-rayed."

Ricky was ushered to his seat. Katy, sporting her new eyeglasses, offered to hold the ice bag in place, and Mack's brothers began sharing stories about all their rodeo injuries.

Beth's eyes burned as she took in the scene.

"Kids break bones." Mack hugged her. "It's nothing to cry over."

"That's not why I'm crying." She gazed into Mack's sexy brown eyes. "I'm crying because I almost walked away from this." She swept her arm in front of her. "You, your family, Ricky and Katy. The chance to be a mother."

"I wouldn't have let you." Mack kissed the top of her head. "No way was I going to ride herd over Ricky and Katy on my own."

Mack was just saying that. Without a doubt he would have raised the kids as a single father and done a fantastic job. Beth was humbled and blessed that he'd chosen her to help him. "I love you, Mack."

"I know, darlin'."

She pinched his side.

"Hey, what's that for?"

"Thank you for showing me that 'Love Don't Hurt Every Time.'"

"Quoting Haggard songs, are you?" He lowered his head, and right before his mouth touched hers he whispered, "'There Won't Be Another Now.'"

* * * * *

Porter is the last Cash brother left single!
Be sure to look for the final book in Marin Thomas's
CASH BROTHERS *miniseries in early 2015!*

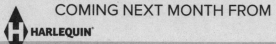
#1509 HER FOREVER COWBOY
Forever, Texas
by Marie Ferrarella

Leaving her city life—and a bad fiancé—behind, Dr. Alisha Cordell shows up in Forever, Texas. The move is temporary...that is until she meets Brett Murphy, a charming cowboy who has every intention of convincing her to stay!

#1514 THE TEXAN'S TWINS
Texas Rodeo Barons
by Pamela Britton

Rodeo cowboy Jet Baron can't stop thinking about Jasmine Marks. But when he learns she's a single mom of twin girls, he thinks he might be in over his head!

#1515 THE SURPRISE TRIPLETS
Safe Harbor Medical
by Jacqueline Diamond

Melissa and Edmond's marriage ended because he didn't want children. Years later, he is appointed the guardian to his seven-year-old niece and needs his ex's help—only to find Melissa's pregnant...with triplets!

#1516 COWBOY IN THE MAKING
by Julie Benson

While recovering from an injury on his grandfather's ranch, city boy Jamie Westland is drawn to Emma Donovan. But can this wannabe cowboy find happiness with a country gal?

REQUEST YOUR FREE BOOKS!
2 FREE NOVELS PLUS 2 FREE GIFTS!

HARLEQUIN®

American ★ Romance®

LOVE, HOME & HAPPINESS

HAR13R

"You going to take off your dress now? Or later?"

The woman's eyes widened. *"Excuse me?"*

"Don't worry. My friends didn't know I was meeting a man. A project engineer, actually, and you don't exactly look the part. Nice try, though."

"Let me guess—Jet Baron."

"One and the same." He gave her a welcoming smile, his gaze slowly sliding over her body.

"Why am I *not* surprised?" she asked.

Her sarcasm startled him, as did the way she eyed him up and down. So direct. So appraising. So…disappointed.

He straightened. "If you're going to start stripping, you better do it now. I'm expecting the engineer at any moment."

"You think I'm some kind of prank. An actress hired to, what? Pretend to have a meeting with you? Then strip out of my clothes?"

He was starting to get a funny feeling. "Well, yeah."

She took a step toward him, and he would be lying if he didn't feel as if, somehow, the joke was on him.

"Tell me something, what makes you think the engineer in question is a man?"

"I was told that."

"By whom?"

"I don't know who told me, I just know he's a man. All engineers in the oil industry are men."

She took another step toward him. "There are actually quite a few women in the business. I graduated from Berkley with a degree in geology." She took yet another step closer. "I interned for the USGS out of Menlo Park then moved back to Texas to get my master's in engineering. My father was a wildcatter, and it was from him that I learned the business—so let me reassure you, Mr. Baron, I can tell the difference between an injection hose and a drill pipe. But if you still insist only men can be engineers, perhaps we should call your sister, Lizzie, who hired me."

Jet couldn't speak for a moment. "Oh, crap."

Her extraordinary blue eyes scanned him, her derision clearly evident. "Still want me to strip?"

He almost said yes, but he could tell that he was in enough trouble as it is. "I take it you're J.C.?"

"I am."

"I should apologize."

"You think?"

Look for THE TEXAN'S TWINS
by Pamela Britton next month from
Harlequin® American Romance®.

You Can't Hide in Forever

The minute he lays eyes on Forever's new doctor, Brett Murphy knows the town—and he—won't be the same. Alisha Cordell is raising the temperature of every male within miles. But the big-city blonde isn't looking to put down roots. The saloon owner and rancher will just have to change the reticent lady doc's mind.

A week after she caught her fiancé cheating, Alisha was on a train headed for a Texas town that was barely a blip on the map. So she's stunned at how fast the place is growing on her. That includes the sexy cowboy with the sassy smile and easygoing charm. Brett's also been burned by love, but he's eager for a second chance…with Alisha. Is she ready to make Brett—and Forever— part of her long-term plans?

Look for
Her Forever Cowboy
by *USA TODAY* bestselling author
MARIE FERRARELLA
from the *Forever, Texas* miniseries from
Harlequin® American Romance®.

Available September 2014
wherever books and ebooks are sold.

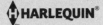

HARLEQUIN®

American Romance®

A Little Bit Country...

Emma Donovan ran off to Nashville when she was
young and full of dreams. Now she's back home in
Colorado with a little more common sense.
And that sense is telling her not to count on
Jamie Westland. He won't be around long—not
with his big-time career in New York City.

Jamie's never felt at home, not with his adopted family,
not with himself. Now, on his grandfather's ranch,
the pieces of his life are coming together in a way that
feels right. And Emma has so much to do with it.
But when an opportunity comes along back in New York,
he has to decide between his old life and the promise
of a new one...with Emma.

Cowboy in the Making

by JULIE BENSON

Available September 2014
wherever books and ebooks are sold.